PENGUIN CLASSICS
Maigret's Doubts

'Extraordinary masterpieces of the twentieth century'

– John Banville

'A brilliant writer'

– India Knight

'Intense atmosphere and resonant detail . . . make Simenon's fiction remarkably like life' – Julian Barnes

'A truly wonderful writer . . . marvellously readable – lucid, simple, absolutely in tune with the world he creates'

– Muriel Spark

'Few writers have ever conveyed with such a sure touch, the bleakness of human life' – A. N. Wilson

'Compelling, remorseless, brilliant' – John Gray

'A writer of genius, one whose simplicity of language creates indelible images that the florid stylists of our own day can only dream of' – *Daily Mail*

'The mysteries of the human personality are revealed in all their disconcerting complexity' – Anita Brookner

'One of the greatest writers of our time' – *The Sunday Times*

'I love reading Simenon. He makes me think of Chekhov'

– William Faulkner

'One of the great psychological novelists of this century'

– *Independent*

'The greatest of all, the most genuine novelist we have had in literature' – André Gide

'Simenon ought to be spoken of in the same b̶ ̶ as Camu . . . *unday*

Georges Simenon was born on 12 February 1903 in Liège, Belgium, and died in 1989 in Lausanne, Switzerland, where he had lived for the latter part of his life. Between 1931 and 1972 he published seventy-five novels and twenty-eight short stories featuring Inspector Maigret.

Simenon always resisted identifying himself with his famous literary character, but acknowledged that they shared an important characteristic:

> My motto, to the extent that I have one, has been noted often enough, and I've always conformed to it. It's the one I've given to old Maigret, who resembles me in certain points . . . 'understand and judge not'.

Penguin is publishing the entire series of Maigret novels.

GEORGES SIMENON

Maigret's Doubts

Translated by SHAUN WHITESIDE

PENGUIN BOOKS

PENGUIN CLASSICS

UK | USA | Canada | Ireland | Australia
India | New Zealand | South Africa

Penguin Books is part of the Penguin Random House group of companies
whose addresses can be found at global.penguinrandomhouse.com.

First published in French as *Les scrupules de Maigret* by Presses de la Cité 1958
This translation first published 2018
001

Set in 12.5/15 pt Dante MT Std
Typeset by Jouve (UK), Milton Keynes
Printed in Great Britain by Clays Ltd, St Ives plc

ISBN: 978–0–141–98589–3

www.greenpenguin.co.uk

Contents

1. The Tuesday Morning Visitor

It hardly happens more than once or twice a year at Quai des Orfèvres, and sometimes it is over so quickly that you haven't time to notice it: all of a sudden, after a frantic period in which there is a rapid succession of cases, arriving three or four at a time, putting all the staff on edge, so much so that the inspectors, for want of sleep, end up gaunt and red-eyed, all of a sudden there is dead calm, a void, one might say, barely punctuated by some unimportant phone calls.

The same had been true the previous day. Admittedly that had been a Monday, a day that was usually less busy than the others anyway. The same atmosphere prevailed on Tuesday, at eleven o'clock in the morning. In the vast corridor, barely two or three small-time informers hung about uneasily, coming to pass on their information, and all the people in the inspectors' office were at their desks except the ones who were off with flu.

Whereas in an emergency Maigret usually didn't have enough staff and had a huge amount of trouble finding enough men to put on a case, today he could have had access to almost his entire squad.

It is true that it was more or less the same in the rest of Paris. It was 10 January. After the holidays, people were living their lives in slow motion, with a vague hangover, and the prospect of rents and taxes to be paid.

The sky, in harmony with everyone's minds and moods, was a neutral grey, the same grey, more or less, as the flagstones. It was cold, not cold enough to be picturesque or newsworthy, but an irritating cold, nothing more than that, the kind of cold you only noticed after walking in the streets for a certain amount of time.

The radiators in the offices were scorching, adding to the thickness of the atmosphere, with occasional gurgles in the pipes and strange noises issuing from the boiler.

Like schoolchildren once the exams are over, some addressed themselves to the small jobs that are normally put off until later, discovering in drawers forgotten reports, statistics to be established, dull administrative tasks.

Almost all the people who made the headlines were on the Côte d'Azur or on the ski slopes.

If Maigret had still had his coal-fired stove, which he had been allowed to keep for so long after the installation of central heating, but which had finally been taken away, he would have broken off from time to time to refill and poke it, bringing down a rain of red ash.

He wasn't in a bad mood, but he wasn't in very good form either, and in the bus that brought him from Boulevard Richard-Lenoir he had wondered for a moment if he wasn't coming down with flu.

Perhaps it was his wife he was worried about? The previous day his friend Pardon, the doctor on Rue Picpus, had phoned him out of the blue.

'Hello! Maigret . . . Don't tell Madame Maigret that I've let you know.'

'Let me know what?'

'She came to see me just now and insisted that I wasn't to talk to you about it . . .'

Less than a year before, Maigret had gone to see Pardon as well, asking him not to tell his wife about his visit.

'Most importantly, don't be anxious. I examined her carefully. There's nothing serious . . .'

The previous day, when he took the call, Maigret had been as lethargic as he was this morning, with the same administrative report to complete.

'What did she say was wrong with her?'

'For some time she's been breathless when climbing the stairs, and particularly in the morning her legs feel heavy. Nothing to worry about, I should tell you again. Except that her circulation isn't quite what it should be. I prescribed her some pills to be taken after each meal. I should also tell you, so that you aren't surprised, that I've put her on a diet. I would like her to lose five or six kilos, which would take the strain off her heart.'

'You're sure that . . .'

'I swear that there's absolutely nothing to worry about, but I thought it was better to put you in the picture. If you want my advice, pretend not to notice a thing. What scares her most is the idea that you might worry on her account . . .'

Knowing his wife, she would have gone to buy her medication from the nearest chemist. The phone call was in the morning. At lunchtime he had watched Madame Maigret, who hadn't taken any pills in front of him. Not in the evening either. He had looked for a little bottle, or a box, in the drawers in the sideboard and then, as if he wasn't doing anything, in the kitchen.

Where had she hidden her medication? She had eaten less than usual; she hadn't had any pudding, in spite of her sweet tooth.

'I think I'm going to go on a bit of a diet,' she had said, joking. 'I'm starting to split my dresses . . .'

He trusted Pardon. He stayed calm. But it did weigh on his mind, or more exactly it made him melancholy.

The previous year he had been the first to have three weeks of complete rest. It was his wife's turn now. That meant that they were very slowly reaching the age of minor ailments, of little repairs that needed carrying out, a little like cars which suddenly need to go to the garage almost every week.

Except that you can buy replacement parts for cars. You can even put in a new engine.

When the clerk knocked on his door and opened it as usual without waiting for an answer, Maigret was not aware of his ruminations. He lifted his head from his dossier and looked at old Joseph with big, sleepy-looking eyes.

'What is it?'

'Someone insists on seeing you in person.'

And Joseph, who didn't make a sound when he walked, set down a form on the corner of the desk.

Maigret read a name written in pencil, but since the name meant nothing to him he paid it no attention. He would only remember that it was a two-syllable surname probably beginning with an M. Only the first name stayed in his memory, Xavier, because it was the name of his first boss at Quai des Orfèvres, old Xavier Guichard.

Beneath the printed words: 'object of visit', it said something like: 'absolutely needs to talk to Detective Chief Inspector Maigret'.

Joseph waited impassively. It was grey enough in the office for the lamps to be lit, but Maigret hadn't thought of lighting them.

'Will you see him?'

He replied with a movement of his head and a slight shrug. Why not? A moment later, a man of about forty was brought in. He had an unremarkable face and might have been any one of the thousands of men one sees at six o'clock in the evening, hurrying towards the nearest Métro.

'I'm sorry to disturb you, detective chief inspector . . .'

'Have a seat.'

His visitor was slightly nervous, but not excessively so, more emotional, like so many who came into this very office. He wore a dark overcoat, which he unbuttoned before sitting down, keeping his hat on his knees at first and then, a little later, placing it on the carpet by his feet.

Then he smiled mechanically, probably a sign of shyness. After giving a little cough, he said:

'The most difficult thing, I'm sure you'll agree, is where to start. Of course, like everyone, I have said heaven knows how many times in my head the things that I am about to tell you, but when the time comes it all turns into a blur . . .'

Another smile, seeking approval or encouragement

from the inspector. But Maigret's interest had not yet been aroused. The man had come at a bad time, when his mind was still drowsy.

'You must receive many visits of the same kind, people coming to tell you about their small troubles, convinced that you will find them interesting.'

He had brown hair, he wasn't bad-looking, although his nose was a little crooked and his lower lip was a bit too fleshy.

'I can assure you that that isn't the case with me and that I hesitated for a long time before disturbing a man as busy as you are.'

He must have expected a desk covered with files, with two or three telephones ringing at the same time, inspectors going in and out, witnesses or suspects slumped on the chairs. And that was more or less what he would have found on another day, but his disenchantment didn't raise a smile from Maigret, whose mind seemed to be quite blank.

In fact, looking at the man's suit, he was thinking that it was made of a good material and must have been cut by a local tailor. A grey suit, almost black. Black shoes. A neutral tie.

'Let me assure you, inspector, that I'm not insane. I don't know if you know Doctor Steiner, Place Denfert-Rochereau. He's a neurologist, which is, I believe, more or less synonymous with psychiatrist, and he has acted several times as an expert witness in court trials.'

Maigret's thick eyebrows rose slightly, but not exaggeratedly.

'Have you been to see Steiner?'

'I went to ask him for a consultation, yes, and I should mention in passing that his consultations last an hour and that he leaves nothing to chance. He found nothing. He considers me completely normal. As for my wife, who didn't go and see him . . .'

He paused, because his monologue was not exactly the one he had prepared, and he was struggling to remember it word for word. With a mechanical gesture he had taken a pack of cigarettes from his pocket but didn't dare to ask permission to smoke.

'You may,' Maigret said.

'Thank you.'

His fingers were slightly clumsy. He was nervous.

'Excuse me. I should control myself better than that. I can't help being emotional. It's the first time that I've seen you in the flesh, all of a sudden, in your office, with your pipes . . .'

'May I ask you what your profession is?'

'I should have started with that. It isn't a very common one, and like many people you may smile. I work at the Grands Magasins du Louvre on Rue de Rivoli. Officially, my title is first salesman in the toy department. That is to say that I was kept on my toes during the holiday season. In fact, I have a specialism that takes up most of my activity: I look after the train sets.'

He seemed to be forgetting the purpose of his visit and where he was and instead was talking freely about his favourite subject.

'Did you walk past the Magasins du Louvre in December?'

Maigret said neither yes nor no. He couldn't remember. He vaguely remembered a giant decoration in lights on the façade, but he couldn't have said what the moving and multi-coloured characters represented.

'If you did, you saw, in the third window on the Rue de Rivoli, a precise reconstruction of Gare Saint-Lazare, with all its platforms, its suburban and express trains, its signals, its signal boxes. It took me three months of work, and I had to go to Switzerland and Germany to buy some of the material. That may seem childish to you, but if I told you our turnover on train sets alone . . . Most importantly, don't imagine that our clientele consists only of children. Some grown-ups, including men in important positions, are passionate about train sets, and I am often called to people's houses to . . .'

He broke off again.

'Am I boring you?'

'No.'

'Are you listening to me?'

Maigret nodded. His visitor must have been between forty and forty-five, and wore a red-gold wedding ring, broad and flat, almost the same as the one the inspector was wearing. He also wore a tie-pin representing a railway signal.

'I can't remember where I got to. I didn't come to see you to talk to you about train sets, of course, and I realize that I'm wasting your time. And yet you need to be able to place me, don't you? You need me to tell you that I live on Avenue de Châtillon, near the church of Saint-Pierre de Montrouge, in the fourteenth arrondissement, and that

I have lived in the same accommodation for eighteen years. No: nineteen . . . Well, it will be nineteen years in March . . . I'm married . . .'

He was sorry not to be clearer, and sorry that he had to give too many details. It seemed as if when the ideas came to him he weighed them up, wondered whether they were important or not, then expressed or rejected them.

He looked at his watch.

'It's precisely because I'm married . . .'

He smiled apologetically.

'It would be easier if you asked the questions, but you can't, because you don't know what it's about . . .'

Maigret almost blamed himself for being so static. It wasn't his fault. It was physical. He was struggling to take an interest in what he was being told, and regretted allowing Joseph to show the visitor in.

'I'm listening . . .'

He filled a pipe to keep himself busy and glanced at the window, beyond which there was only pale grey. It looked like a worn-out backcloth from a provincial theatre.

'Above all I must stress that I am not accusing anyone, inspector. I love my wife. We've been married for twelve years, Gisèle and I, and we have hardly ever argued. I talked to Doctor Steiner about it, after he examined me, and he said to me solicitously, "I would be obliged if you would bring your wife to see me." Except, on what pretext can I ask Gisèle to follow me to see a neurologist? I can't even claim that she is mad, because she gets on with her work, and no one has any complaints.

'You see, I'm not a very educated person. I grew up in

9

care and had to educate myself, and I consider that knowledge is man's most precious property.

'Forgive me for talking to you like this. It is to explain to you at last that when Gisèle started behaving differently towards me, I went to libraries, including the Bibliothèque Nationale, to consult books that would have been too expensive for me to buy. Besides, my wife would have been worried if she had found them at home . . .'

To prove that he was more or less following this chatter, Maigret asked:

'Books about psychiatry?'

'Yes. I don't claim to have understood everything. Most of them are written in a language that is too complicated for me. But I did find books on neuroses and psychoses that made me think. I imagine you know the difference between neuroses and psychoses? I've also studied schizophrenia, but I think in all conscience that her condition doesn't go quite that far . . .'

Maigret thought of his wife, of Doctor Pardon, and observed a little brown mole in the corner of his visitor's lip.

'If I understand correctly, you suspect your wife of not being in her normal state of mind?'

The moment had come, and the man paled slightly and gulped back his saliva two or three times before declaring, as if searching for his words and weighing their meaning:

'I am convinced that for several months, five or six at least, my wife has been planning to kill me. That, inspector, is why I came to see you in person. I have no formal proof, or else I would have started with that. I am prepared to give you all the clues I have, which fall into two categories. Psychological clues first of all, the most difficult to expose, as you must understand because most of them are trivial facts which have no significance in themselves, but which cumulatively assume a meaning.

'As to material clues, there is one, which I have brought you, and which is the most troubling . . .'

He opened his overcoat, his waistcoat, pulled his wallet from his inside pocket and took out a folded paper of the kind in which some chemists still put headache powders.

The paper did contain powder, a powder of a dirty white colour.

'I will leave you this specimen, which you can send for analysis. Before coming to you, I asked for it to be analysed by a salesman at the Louvre who is a passionate chemist and who has set up a real laboratory. He was categorical. It is white phosphide. Not phosphate, as you might think, but phosphide, I checked in the dictionary. And not just the Larousse. I also consulted textbooks on chemistry. White phosphide is an almost colourless powder, which is extremely toxic. It was used in the old days, in minute doses, as a remedy for certain illnesses and it was abandoned precisely because of its toxicity.'

He paused, slightly disoriented at having in front of him a Maigret who was still impassive and apparently miles away.

'My wife doesn't do chemistry. She isn't following a course of treatment. She has none of the illnesses for which one might, in extremis, prescribe zinc phosphide. And yet

I didn't find just a few grams at home, but a bottle containing at least fifty grams. And I happened upon it by chance. On the ground floor of our house I have a kind of studio where I work on the models for my window displays and carry out minor mechanical tests. They are just toys, of course, but as I have said, toys represent . . .'

'I know.'

'One day when my wife was out, I knocked over a pot of glue on my workbench. I opened the cupboard where we keep the brooms and cleaning products. Looking for a detergent of some kind, I happened to lay my hand on a small unlabelled bottle that seemed to me to be a strange shape.

'Now, if you connect this discovery with the fact that over the last few months I have had, for the first time in my life, a number of anxieties that I have told Doctor Steiner about . . .'

The phone on the desk rang, and Maigret picked it up, recognizing the voice of the commissioner of the Police Judiciaire.

'Is that you, Maigret? Have you got a few minutes? I'd like to introduce you to an American criminologist who is in my office and very keen to shake your hand . . .'

Once he had hung up again, Maigret looked around. There was nothing confidential lying about on the desk. His visitor didn't have the look of a dangerous man.

'Will you excuse me? I'll only be a few minutes.'

'Be my guest . . .'

But at the door he had a sudden reflex and crossed the office once more to open, as he usually did, the door of the inspectors' office. But he gave them no special instruction. It didn't occur to him.

A few minutes later he pushed open the chief's padded door. A big red-haired man got out of an armchair and shook his hand vigorously, saying in French with the merest hint of an accent:

'It's a great joy for me to see you in the flesh, Monsieur Maigret. When you came to my country I missed you, because I was in San Francisco, and you didn't come all the way to us. My friend Fred Ward, who welcomed you in New York and went with you to Washington, has told me exciting things about you.'

The commissioner gestured to Maigret to sit down.

'I hope I'm not disturbing you in the middle of one of those interrogations that seem so strange to us Americans?'

The inspector reassured him. The chief's guest held out his cigarettes and then changed his mind.

'I forgot that you are a fan of the pipe.'

It happened periodically, and it was always the same phrases, the same questions, the same exaggerated and embarrassing admiration. Maigret, who hated being examined as if he were a freak, put a brave face on things and at such moments he had a special smile that greatly amused his chief.

One question led to another. They discussed technique, then talked about some famous cases, on which he had to supply an opinion.

Inevitably the conversation turned to his methods, something that always strained his patience, because, as he repeated, without managing to destroy the legend, he had never had any methods.

To rescue him, the commissioner rose to his feet, saying:

'Now, if you would like to go upstairs and visit our museum . . .'

It was part of every visit of this kind, and, with his hands crushed once more by a more vigorous grip than his own, Maigret was able to return to his office.

He stopped, surprised, in the doorway, because there was no one sitting in the armchair that he had offered his train-set salesman. The office was empty, with only some cigarette smoke floating just below the ceiling.

He went into the inspectors' office.

'Has he left?'

'Who?'

Janvier and Lucas were playing cards, which they did barely three times a year, except when they were on guard duty all night.

'Nothing . . . It doesn't matter . . .'

He went out into the corridor, where old Joseph was reading the paper.

'Has my client left?'

'Not long ago. He came out of your office and told me he couldn't wait any longer, that he absolutely had to get back to the shop, where they were waiting for him. Should I have . . . ?'

'No. It doesn't matter.'

The man was free to go, since no one had asked him to come.

It was at that moment that Maigret realized he had forgotten the man's name.

'I don't suppose, Joseph, that you remember what his name is?'

'I must confess, inspector, that I didn't look at his form.'

Maigret went back to his office and immersed himself once again in his report, which contained nothing exciting. The boiler must have been racing, because the radiators had never been so scorching, and were making worrying noises. He nearly got up to turn the handle, but he couldn't be bothered and instead reached for the telephone.

His plan was to call the Magasins du Louvre and find out about the head of the toy department. But if he did that wouldn't they wonder why the police were suddenly interested in one of the members of staff? Didn't Maigret risk damaging his visitor's reputation?

He worked a little longer and picked up the receiver almost mechanically.

'Could you try and find me a certain Doctor Steiner, who lives on Place Denfert-Rochereau?'

Less than ten minutes later the phone rang.

'You've got Doctor Steiner on the line.'

'Forgive me for disturbing you, doctor . . . This is Maigret . . . The detective chief inspector at the Police Judiciaire, yes . . . I think you recently had a patient whose first name is Xavier and whose surname escapes me . . .'

The doctor, at the other end of the line, didn't seem to remember.

'He works in toys . . . Train sets, to be specific . . . He

said he went to see you to check that he wasn't insane and then talked to you about his wife . . .'

'Just one moment. Will you excuse me? I will have to consult my files.'

Maigret heard him saying to someone, 'Mademoiselle Berthe, would you be so kind . . .'

He must have moved away from the phone, because there was nothing to be heard, and the silence lasted for quite a while, so long that Maigret thought they had been cut off.

Judging by his voice, Steiner was a cold man, probably vain, at least with a strong sense of his own importance.

'May I ask you, inspector, why you called me?'

'Because this gentleman was in my office just now and left before our discussion was over. But the fact is that while I was listening to him I tore the form on which he had written his name into little pieces.'

'Did you call him in?'

'No.'

'What is he suspected of doing?'

'Nothing. He came of his own accord to tell me his story.'

'Has anything happened?'

'I don't think so. He spoke to me about certain fears which I think he may have told you about.'

Ninety-nine doctors in a hundred would have been cooperative by this point; Maigret had landed upon one who wasn't.

'You know, I assume,' Steiner said, 'that patient confidentiality prevents me from . . .'

'I'm not asking you, doctor, to betray patient confidentiality. I am asking you, first of all, for the surname of this man Xavier. I could find it easily by phoning the Grands Magasins du Louvre, where he works, but I thought that if I did so I would risk putting him in a bad light with his employers.'

'That is quite likely, I grant you.'

'I also know that he lives on Avenue de Châtillon, and my men, if they questioned the concierges, would reach the same result. In that way too we might prejudice your patient by causing a fuss.'

'I understand.'

'So?'

'His name is Marton, Xavier Marton,' the neurologist said reluctantly.

'When did he come to see you?'

'I think I can answer that question as well. About three weeks ago, on 21 December, to be precise . . .'

'So just as he was at his busiest with the Christmas holidays. I expect he was rather agitated?'

'Meaning?'

'Listen, doctor, once again, I'm not asking you to give away a secret. We have, as you know, expeditious means of acquiring information.'

Silence at the other end, a disapproving silence, Maigret could have sworn. Doctor Steiner mustn't have been very fond of the police.

'Xavier Marton, since that is his name,' Maigret went on, 'acted like a normal man in my office. And yet . . .'

The doctor repeated:

'And yet?'

'I'm no psychiatrist, and after listening to him I would like to know whether I was dealing with an unbalanced person or . . .'

'What would you call an unbalanced person?'

Maigret was flushed and held the receiver in a tight and menacing grip.

'You have responsibilities, doctor, and you are bound to a rule of patient confidentiality which I am not attempting to lead you to infringe in any way, but we too have responsibilities of our own. I don't like to think that I let a man leave who might, tomorrow . . .'

'I let him leave my office too.'

'So you don't think he's a madman?'

Another silence.

'What do you think about what he told you about his wife? When he was here he didn't have time to get to the end of his story . . .'

'I haven't examined his wife.'

'And from what he told you, you have no idea of . . .'

'No idea.'

'You have nothing to add?'

'Nothing, I'm sorry to say. Will you excuse me? I have a client who is getting impatient.'

Maigret put the phone down as if he wanted to break the receiver over the doctor's head.

Then, almost immediately, his rage subsided, and he shrugged his shoulders, even smiling in the end.

'Janvier!' he called so that he could be heard from the next room.

'Yes, chief.'

'I want you to go to the Grands Magasins du Louvre and go upstairs to the toy section. Pretend to be a customer. Look for a man who is supposed to be the head of the department, between forty and forty-five, dark hair, with a hairy mole to the left of his lip.'

'What should I ask him?'

'Nothing. If the head of department answers to that description, his name is Xavier Marton, and that's all I want to know. In fact, while you're there, pretend to take an interest in train sets as a way of getting him to speak. Observe him. That's all.'

'Is that who you were talking about on the phone a moment ago?'

'Yes. Did you hear?'

'You want to know if he's mad?'

Maigret merely shrugged. On any other day, he might not have worried for more than a few minutes about Marton's visit. At the Police Judiciaire they are used to receiving madmen and semi-madmen, lunatics, fantasists, individuals, both male and female, who think they have been chosen to save the world from perdition, and others who are convinced that mysterious enemies are after their lives or their secrets.

The Crime Squad, or 'Homicide', as it is currently known, is not a psychiatric hospital and when it does deal with such individuals it is usually only when they have finally broken the law, which thankfully doesn't always happen.

It was almost midday. He thought of phoning Pardon,

said to himself that it wasn't worth it, that in that morning's visit there was nothing more worrying than in a hundred visits of the same kind that he had received.

Why was he thinking about the pills that his wife had to take with each meal? Because of the zinc phosphide that Xavier Marton claimed to have found in the broom cupboard. Where did Madame Maigret hide her pills so as not to worry her husband?

Intrigued, he vowed to look everywhere. She had probably spent a long time coming up with a clever hiding place that he wouldn't think of.

He would see. In the meantime, he closed his file, went at last to turn the radiator halfway down and wondered whether he should leave the window open during the lunch hour.

As he left, he noticed the sachet of white powder on his desk and took it to Lucas.

'Pass this on to the laboratory. Ask them to let me know what it is this afternoon.'

On the embankment the cold caught him unawares, and he turned up the collar of his overcoat, plunged his hands into his pockets and headed for the bus stop. He didn't like Doctor Steiner at all and he was thinking more about him than about the train-set specialist.

2. The Insurance Agent

As had been the case for years and years, he didn't need to knock on the door. It opened as soon as he put his feet on the mat, and he didn't remember ringing the bell.

'You're home early,' his wife observed.

And all of a sudden she frowned very slightly, as she did when she saw that he was worried. In that she was never mistaken. She could spot the slightest change in his mood and, although she didn't ask him direct questions, she still tried to guess what it was that was troubling him.

And yet, for now, it wasn't the visit of the man with the train sets. He might have been thinking about him on the bus, but what had just given him a concerned and slightly melancholy expression was a memory that had risen to the surface while he paused on the second-floor landing. The previous winter, the old woman who lived above them had said, when he bumped into her in front of the concierge's lodge and touched his hat:

'You should see a doctor, Monsieur Maigret.'

'Do you think I look ill?'

'No. I haven't even noticed. It's your footstep on the stairs. For some time now it has been getting heavier, and you seem to pause every four or five steps.'

It wasn't because of her that he had gone to see Pardon some weeks later, but she was still right. Was he going to explain to his wife that it was that memory that made him seem very distant?

She hadn't yet laid the table. As usual, he paced about the dining room and the sitting room and, almost unconsciously, began opening the drawers, lifting the lid of the sewing chest and a red lacquered box in which they kept unimportant objects.

'Are you looking for something?'

'No.'

He was looking for the medicine. He was very intrigued. He wondered if he would end up finding the hiding place.

And yes, in the end, it was true that he didn't have his usual energy. Didn't he have the right, like everyone else, to be sulky on a cold, grey winter day? He had been like that since the morning, and it wasn't all that unpleasant. You can appear grumpy without being unhappy.

He didn't like his wife darting furtive little glances at him. It made him feel guilty, when in fact he wasn't guilty in the slightest. What could he have said to reassure her? That Pardon had told him about her visit?

In fact he was only just beginning to realize that he was annoyed, indeed a little sad. It was because of the man who had come to see him that morning. It was the kind of intimate little secret that he couldn't confide in anyone and didn't like to confess to himself.

That fellow, train-set specialist though he might have been, wasn't a pain in the neck of the kind that so often passed through Quai des Orfèvres. He had a problem. He had chosen to talk about it frankly to Maigret. Not to just any policeman. To Maigret.

And yet, when Maigret had gone back to his office after going to the chief's office to meet the American, Xavier Marton was gone.

He had left without taking his confidences to their conclusion. Why? Was he in a hurry? Or was he perhaps disappointed?

Before coming to see Maigret, he had formed a precise idea about him. He must have expected understanding, immediate human contact. The person he had found was someone rather listless, dulled by the suffocating heat of the radiators, who looked at him without much encouragement and wore a gloomy or bored expression.

It was nothing, though. Just a fleeting shadow. Soon he would stop thinking about it. And when he was at the table he made a point of talking about something completely different.

'Don't you think it's time to get a maid? There's a room we've never used on the sixth floor . . .'

'What would she do?'

'The housework, good heavens! The heavy work, let's say.'

He would have been wise not to approach the subject.

'Is there something wrong with your lunch?'

'No, it's fine. But you're wearing yourself out.'

'I have a woman to do the cleaning two days a week. Can you tell me how I would spend my days if I had a maid?'

'You could go for a walk.'

'All on my own?'

'There's nothing to stop you having friends.'

Right! Now it was his wife's turn to be sad. In her mind it was a bit as if he wanted to take away one of her prerogatives, the one closest to her heart.

'Do you think I'm getting old?'

'We're all getting old. That's not what I mean. I thought . . .'

There are days like this when you get everything wrong, with the best will in the world. Once they had finished lunch, he dialled a number. A familiar voice replied. He said:

'Is that you, Pardon?'

And he realized that he had committed yet another pointless act of cruelty. His wife was looking at him, frightened, saying to herself that he had discovered her secret . . .

'Maigret here . . .'

'Is something wrong?'

'No, I'm fine . . .'

He hurried to add:

'And so is my wife . . . So tell me, are you very busy?'

Pardon's remark made him smile. It was funny, because he too could have said exactly the same thing.

'Dead calm! In November and December everyone decided to fall ill at the same time and I didn't spend three whole nights in my bed. Some days the waiting room was full to bursting, and the phone wouldn't stop ringing. During the holidays, a few hangovers and a few liver disorders. Now that people have spent their money, keeping only what they need for their rent, they're all cured . . .'

'Can I come and see you? I'd like to chat with you about a case that came up at the Police Judiciaire this morning.'

'I'll be here waiting.'

'Now?'

'If you like.'

Madame Maigret asked him:

'Are you sure it's not about you? You don't feel ill?'

'I swear.'

He kissed her then stepped backwards to tap her on the cheeks and murmur:

'Ignore me. I think I got out of the wrong side of bed.'

Without hurrying, he reached Rue Picpus, where Pardon lived in an old building with no lift. The receptionist, who knew him, didn't bring him into the waiting room, but along the corridor and through the back door.

'He'll just be a minute. As soon as his patient comes out, I'll show you in.'

He found Pardon in a white coat, in his surgery with its frosted-glass windows.

'I hope you didn't mention to your wife that I'd told you what was happening? She would be cross with me for the rest of her life.'

'I'm delighted that she's decided to take care of herself. Is it true that there's nothing to worry about?'

'Nothing at all. In a few weeks, in three months, let's say, when she's lost a few kilos, she'll feel ten years younger.'

Maigret pointed to the waiting room.

'Am I not taking up your patients' time?'

'There are only two of them, and they have nothing else to do.'

'Do you know a certain Doctor Steiner?'

'The neurologist?'

'Yes. He lives on Place Denfert-Rochereau.'

'I vaguely knew him at the Faculty, because he's about my age, and then I lost touch with him. But I've heard my colleagues talking about him. He's one of the most brilliant minds of his generation. After passing all his exams with flying colours, he was first a trainee, then departmental head at Sainte-Anne's Hospital. Then he passed his senior teaching diploma, and everyone expected him to become one of the youngest professors in the Faculty.'

'What happened?'

'Nothing. It's his character. Perhaps he has an exaggerated sense of his own worth. He lets you know about it, he can be brusque, almost arrogant. At the same time he's a troubled soul, for whom every case presents moral problems. During the war he refused to wear the yellow star, claiming that he didn't have a drop of Jewish blood. The Germans proved the opposite in the end and sent him to a concentration camp. He came back embittered and imagines that his progress has been thwarted because of his origins, which is crazy, because there are several Jewish professors at the Faculty. Have you had dealings with him?'

'I called him this morning. I wanted to get some information out of him, but now I understand that it's pointless to insist.'

A bit like the man who came to see him this morning, Maigret didn't know where to start.

'Even though it isn't your specialization, I would like to ask your opinion about a story that someone told me just now. I had a man in his forties in my office. He seemed normal and talked to me calmly, without exaggerating, measuring his words. He's been married for about twelve years, if I remember correctly, and he's been living for longer than that on Avenue Châtillon.'

Pardon, who had lit a cigarette, was listening attentively.

'He works with electric trains.'

'You mean he's a railway engineer?'

'No, I mean toy train sets.'

Pardon frowned.

'I know,' Maigret said. 'I was struck by that too. But he doesn't do it as a hobby. He is the head salesman in the toy department of a large store, and it was he who, among other things, set up the train set for the Christmas window display. As far as I can tell he's in reasonably good health.'

'What crime has he committed?'

'None. At least that's what I assume. He told me that his wife has been trying to kill him for some time.'

'How did he become aware of that?'

'He left before he could give me any details. From what I can tell, hidden in a cupboard for brooms and cleaning products he found a little bottle containing a considerable quantity of zinc phosphide.'

Pardon grew more attentive.

'He was the one who analysed the product and he seems to have carried out an in-depth study of zinc phosphide. He even brought me a sample.'

'Do you want to know if it's a poison?'

'I assume it's a toxic product.'

'Very toxic. In some areas it's used to kill voles. Has he been ill?'

'Off colour, several times.'

'Did he report it?'

'No. He disappeared from my office before he could tell me what he was getting at. It's just that I'm worried about it.'

'I think I understand . . . Was he the one who went to see Steiner? With his wife . . . ?'

'No. Alone. He's been seeing the doctor for almost a month, to check . . .'

'. . . that he isn't insane?'

Maigret nodded and took a moment to relight his pipe before continuing:

'I could call him into my office, and even examine him in turn, since Steiner is taking refuge behind patient confidentiality. When I say that I could, I'm exaggerating slightly, because in fact there is nothing to be held against him. He came to see me of his own free will. He told me a story that holds up. Neither he nor anyone else has brought a complaint, and the law doesn't forbid you from possessing a certain quantity of a toxic product. Do you see the problem?'

'Yes, I see.'

'It could be that his story is true. If I go and see his bosses to check on his behaviour, I risk damaging his reputation, because in big stores, as in administrative offices, they are suspicious about people who have attracted the interest of the police. If I question his concierge and his neighbours, rumours will start circulating in his neighbourhood . . .'

'You realize what you're asking of me, Maigret. An opinion about a man I've never seen, and whom you don't really know yourself. And I'm just a family doctor, with only the vaguest notions about neurology and psychiatry.'

'I remember seeing, in your library, a number of books about . . .'

'There is a great chasm between being interested in the subject and formulating a diagnosis. In short, what you would like to know is the reason why he came to tell you his story.'

'That's the first question. He still lives with his wife and seems to have no plans to leave her. He didn't ask me to stop her, or to open an investigation into her. And when I had to leave my office for a few minutes because I was called in to see the chief, he disappeared, as if he didn't want to confide in me any more. Does that suggest anything to you?'

'It might mean all sorts of things. You see, Maigret, back when I was studying, those questions were simpler than they are today. The same is true of medicine as a whole, incidentally, and indeed nearly all the sciences. Whenever an expert was asked in court if a man was mad or of sound mind, the expert usually answered with a yes or a no. Do you read criminological journals?'

'Some.'

'In that case you know as well as I do that it is no longer so easy to make a clear distinction between psychoses, neuroses, psychoneuroses and even, sometimes, schizophrenia. The barrier between a man of sound mind and a psychopath or a neuropath is more and more fragile and, if we were to follow certain foreign scientists . . . But I'm not going to launch off on a scientific or pseudo-scientific dissertation . . .'

'At first sight . . .'

'At first sight, the answer to your question depends on the specialist you are questioning. For example, this business about train sets, even if it is his profession, and remember that he chose it himself, may point to maladjustment, which would in turn suggest psychoneurosis. The fact of coming to see you at Quai des Orfèvres, and obligingly setting out his private life for you would make many a psychiatrist sit up and listen, as would the fact of his going, of his own accord, to see a neurologist to check that he is of sound mind.'

This didn't help Maigret. He had already thought of all these things himself.

'You tell me that he was calm, that he spoke with self-control, without any exaggerated emotion, and that might just as easily be turned against him as considered in his favour, as would having analysed the zinc phosphide and read everything he could about the product. He didn't claim that his wife was going mad?'

'Not exactly. I don't remember every detail. To tell the truth, at first I was only half listening. It was very hot in my office. I was drowsy . . .'

'If he suspects his wife of being insane, that would be another sign. But it's also quite possible that it was his wife who . . .'

Maigret got up from his armchair and started pacing back and forth.

'I would be better off not looking into such things!' he grumbled, as much to himself as to his friend Pardon.

He added straight away:

'And yet I know I will look into it.'

'It's not impossible that all of those things exist only in his imagination, and that he bought the zinc phosphide himself.'

'Is it freely on sale?' Maigret asked.

'No, but the shop where he works may have got hold of some to kill rats, for example.'

'Let's imagine that that's the case, that Marton falls under the category you're thinking of: is he a danger?'

'He could become one at any moment.'

'And let us imagine that his wife is really trying to . . .'

Maigret suddenly turned to the doctor and growled:

'Dammit!'

Then he smiled.

'Excuse me. That wasn't meant for you. Everything was nice and quiet at the office. Just as it is here! The dead season, so to speak. And here's this oddball who shows up with a form, sits down in my office and comes right out and dumps all this responsibility on me . . .'

'You're not responsible.'

'Officially, professionally, no. Which isn't to say that if, tomorrow or next week, one of the two, the man or the woman, commits a crime, I won't be convinced that it was my fault . . .'

'I'm sorry, Maigret, not to be able to help you any

further. Do you want me to try and see Steiner to ask him his opinion?'

Maigret said yes, but without conviction. Pardon called Place Denfert-Rochereau, then the clinic where Steiner was to be found at that time of day. Pardon tried to be humble and respectful, an obscure local doctor speaking to a famous specialist. Maigret could tell from his face and the peremptory tone that he heard vibrating down the receiver that this approach was no more successful than his own.

'He put me in my place.'

'I'm sorry.'

'What for? We had to try. Don't fret too much. If everyone who behaved strangely were to become murderers or victims, you'd find more free apartments than you do today.'

Maigret walked to Place de la République, where he took his bus. At Quai des Orfèvres, Janvier, who was in the inspectors' office, came immediately to give his report, with a sheepish expression.

'He can't have seen me here, can he?' he said. 'And my photograph hasn't exactly been on the front page of the papers. Do I look that much of a policeman?'

In the whole building, Janvier was the one who looked least like a policeman.

'I went up to the toy department and I recognized him straight away from the description you gave me. At work he wears a long grey overall, with the initials of the shop embroidered in red. There was a train set in operation, and I watched it run. Then I gestured to our man and started asking him innocent questions, like a father who wanted to buy a train set for his son. I know what it is, because I bought one for my own boy two Christmases ago. He barely let me say two or three sentences. Then he interrupted me, murmuring, "Tell Inspector Maigret that it isn't very clever on his part to send you here, and that he risks making me lose my job."

'He spoke almost without moving his lips, looking uneasily at a store inspector who was watching us from a distance.'

On Maigret's desk there was a laboratory file, with the words *Zinc phosphide* written in red.

Maigret was close to dropping the case. As he had said to Pardon, or as Pardon had said to him, he couldn't really remember, it didn't concern him from a strictly professional point of view and, if he annoyed Xavier Marton, he might very easily bring a complaint and cause him trouble.

'I'd like to send you to Avenue de Châtillon to question the concierge and the neighbours. Except no one in the area must suspect that the police are looking into our man. You could go door to door selling vacuum cleaners, for example . . .'

Janvier couldn't help pulling a face at the idea of dragging an electric vacuum cleaner from house to house.

'If you prefer, present yourself as an insurance salesman.'

Janvier clearly did prefer that.

'Try and find out how the household lives, what the wife looks like, what people think of her locally. If his wife is at home you can always ring and suggest a life insurance policy . . .'

'I'll do my best, chief.'

The weather was still just as grey, just as cold, and the office was almost freezing, as Maigret had forgotten to turn the radiator back on. He was about to turn the knob when he wondered if he should go and see the chief to ask his advice. If he chose not to, it was for fear of appearing ridiculous. He had realized, as he told the story to Pardon, how little evidence he had.

Slowly filling his pipe, he immersed himself again in the file that he had abandoned that morning, and which no longer interested him. An hour passed. The air became more opaque, because of the smoke and the twilight. He turned on the lamp with the green shade and got up to adjust the radiator, which was overheating again. There was a knock at the door. Old Joseph murmured, setting down a form on the corner of the desk:

'A lady.'

She must have impressed the old clerk for him to use that word.

Joseph added:

'I think it's the wife of that man this morning.'

The name written on the file had reminded him of something: Madame Marton. And underneath it, after 'object of visit', the word 'personal' was written.

'Where is she?'

'In the waiting room. Shall I show her in?'

He nearly said yes, then changed his mind.

'No. I'll deal with her myself.'

He took his time, crossed the inspectors' office, then two more rooms, not emerging into the huge corridor until he had passed the glazed walls of the waiting room. Because it wasn't yet completely dark, the lamps seemed to be casting less light than usual, and the atmosphere was yellowish and sad, like that of a little provincial railway station.

Through the frame of a door he observed the aquarium-like room, in which there were only three people, two of whom must have been there for the Vice Squad: one was a little pimp who stank of Place Pigalle and the other a voluptuous prostitute who had the ease of a regular customer.

They both cast glances at another woman who was waiting, and whose simple but faultless elegance seemed out of place there.

Maigret took his time before reaching the glazed door, which he opened.

'Madame Marton?'

He had noticed the crocodile-skin bag that matched her shoes, the austere suit under a beaver-fur coat.

She got to her feet with exactly the degree of confusion that one might expect of someone who has never had dealings with the police and who suddenly finds herself in front of one of its most important representatives.

'Detective Chief Inspector Maigret?'

The two others, who clearly knew each other, exchanged glances. Maigret brought the lady into his office and showed her to the armchair where her husband had sat that morning.

'I'm sorry to disturb you like this . . .'

She took off her right glove, which was made of soft suede, and crossed her legs.

'I imagine you can guess why I'm here?'

She was the one who went on the attack, and Maigret didn't like that, so he refrained from replying.

'I'm sure you too will talk to me about professional confidentiality . . .'

He was particularly struck by the 'you too'. Did it mean that she had gone to see Doctor Steiner?

It wasn't only her manners that surprised him.

Her husband was certainly not a bad person, and he seemed to earn an honest living. Madame Marton was of a different class. There was nothing fake, nothing vulgar about her elegance, or indeed her confidence.

Even in the waiting room he had noticed the perfect cut of her shoes and her luxurious handbag. Her gloves were of a similar quality, as was the rest of her outfit. Nothing aggressive, nothing studied. Nothing overly obvious. Everything she wore came from excellent fashion houses.

She too seemed to be in her forties, but the forties peculiar to those Parisian women who look after themselves, and both her voice and her attitudes suggested someone at ease everywhere and in all circumstances.

Was there, in fact, a flaw? He thought he was aware of one, a tiny discordant note, but he couldn't put his finger on it. It was an impression more than something he had observed.

'I think, inspector, that we will gain some time if I talk to you frankly. Besides, it would be presumptuous to try and get around a man like you.'

He remained impassive, and either his impassivity didn't trouble her or she had amazing self-control.

'I know my husband came to see you this morning.'

At last Maigret opened his mouth, hoping to disconcert her.

'He told you that?' he asked.

'No. I saw him entering this building and realized that you were the one he was coming to see. He takes an avid interest in all your cases. For years he's been talking about you with great enthusiasm at every opportunity.'

'You mean to say you've been following your husband?'

'Yes,' she admitted simply.

There was a short and slightly embarrassed silence.

'Does that surprise you, having seen and heard him?'

'Do you know what he said to me?'

'I can guess quite easily. We've been married for twelve years, and I know Xavier. He is the most honest, the most courageous, the most winning man in the world. You probably know that he didn't know his parents and was brought up in care?'

He nodded vaguely.

'He was brought up on a farm, in the Sologne, where if he ever managed to get hold of any books they tore them from his hands and burned them. In spite of that he managed to get where he is today and, in my view, he is a long way from having the position he deserves. I'm constantly surprised by the breadth of his knowledge. He has read everything. He knows about everything. And of course, he is exploited. He breaks his back at work. Six months before the holidays he is already preparing for the Christmas season, and it's exhausting for him.'

She had opened her handbag and hesitated to take out a silver cigarette case.

'You may smoke,' he said.

'Thank you. I have this bad habit. I smoke much too much. I hope my presence won't stop you from lighting your pipe?'

He could make out fine crow's feet at the corners of her eyes, but rather than ageing her, they added to her charm. Her greyish blue eyes had the sparkling sweetness of someone slightly short-sighted.

'We must seem ridiculous to you, the two of us, my husband and I, coming to see you one by one as if going to confession. And there is something of that in it. I've been worried about my husband for some time. He is overworked, anxious and has periods of absolute exhaustion during which he doesn't address a word to me.'

Maigret wished that Pardon could have been there, because he might have been able to draw some conclusions.

'As long ago as October . . . yes, in early October . . . I told him he was suffering from nervous exhaustion and that he should consult a doctor . . .'

'Were you the one who talked to him about nervous exhaustion?'

'Yes. Shouldn't I have?'

'Go on.'

'I kept a very close eye on him. He began by complaining about one of his heads of department whom he has never liked. But for the first time he talked about a kind of conspiracy. Then he took against a young salesman . . .'

'For what reason?'

'It sounds ridiculous, but I understand Xavier's reactions a little. I'm not exaggerating if I say that he is the best train-set specialist in the whole of France. I hope that doesn't make you smile? You don't, for example, mock someone who spends his life designing bras or slimming girdles.'

For some reason he asked:

'Do you deal with bras or girdles?'

She laughed.

'I sell them. But this isn't about me. So the new salesman started observing my husband, learning his little tricks, designing circuits . . . In short, he gave him the impression that he was trying to take his place . . . I only really started worrying when I saw that Xavier's fears also extended to me . . .'

'What did he suspect you of?'

'I suppose he told you. It started one evening when, looking at me very intently, he murmured, "You would make a lovely widow, wouldn't you?"

'He would often bring that word up in conversation. For example: "All women are made to be widows. Besides, the statistics show . . ."

'You see the theme. He went on to tell me that without him I would have a wonderful life, that he was the only obstacle to my social rise . . .'

She didn't flinch, in spite of the blank stare that Maigret was deliberately giving her.

'You know the rest. He convinced himself that I had decided to get rid of him. At the dinner table he would sometimes swap my glass for his, without hiding it, in fact staring at me with a mocking look. Before he ate, he would wait for me to swallow the first mouthful. Sometimes, when I came home after him, I would find him searching every corner of the kitchen.

'I don't know what Doctor Steiner could have said to him . . .'

'Did you go with him to see the doctor?'

'No. Xavier announced to me that he was going to see him. That was another act of defiance on his part. He said to me, "I know you're trying to persuade me that I'm going mad. Oh! You're doing it cleverly, drop by drop, in some way. Let's see what a specialist says."'

'Did he tell you the result of the consultation?'

'He never said anything to me, but since then, and it's been about a month now, he's been looking at me with defensive irony. I don't know if you understand what I mean by that. Like a man who has a secret and delights in it. He watches after me. I always have the sense that he's thinking, "Go on, my girl! Do whatever you like. You'll never attain your goal, because I'm on to you . . ."'

Maigret drew on his pipe and asked:

'And you followed him this morning. Are you in the habit of following him?'

'Not every day, no, because I've got a job as well. Usually we leave together, at eight thirty, along Avenue de Châtillon, and we take the same bus to Rue des Pyramides. Then I go to the shop on Rue Saint-Honoré, while he continues down Rue de Rivoli to the Magasins du Louvre. And yet, for some time – I've told you, I think – your name has come up quite often in the conversation. Two days ago he said to me, in a voice that was both sardonic and menacing: "Whatever you do, however clever you are, someone will know."'

She added:

'I understood that you were the one he was alluding to. Even yesterday I followed him to the Magasins du Louvre and stayed there for a certain amount of time keeping watch on the staff entrance, to check that he didn't come out again. This morning I did the same thing . . .'

'And you followed him all the way here?'

She said yes, quite frankly, and leaned forward to stub out her cigarette in the glass ashtray.

'I've tried to give you an idea of the situation. Now I'm ready to answer your questions.'

Only her hands, clutching her crocodile-skin handbag, betrayed a certain nervousness.

3. The Younger Sister from America

In the morning, when he had seemed apathetic and distracted with the train-set salesman, it had been an involuntary apathy which had more to do with drowsiness, a kind of somnolence. Contact had not been established, in short; or more precisely, it had been established too late.

Now, with Madame Marton, he had rediscovered his professional apathy, the one that he had adopted in the past when he was still shy, to disconcert his interlocutors, and which had become an almost unconscious reflex.

She didn't seem impressed and went on looking at him as a child might at a big bear which it doesn't exactly fear, but still keeps checking out of the corner of its eye.

Wasn't she the one who had guided the conversation, finishing with a phrase that Maigret had rarely heard uttered in this office:

'Now, I'm waiting for your questions . . .'

He made her wait for a certain amount of time, allowing silence to settle, deliberately, drawing on his pipe, and at last saying with the air of someone who doesn't really know what he is getting at:

'Why exactly did you come to tell me all this?'

And that threw her, in fact. She began:

'But . . .'

She fluttered her eyelashes, as short-sighted people do, found nothing else to say and smiled faintly to indicate that the answer was obvious.

He went on, like a man who doesn't attach any importance to the matter, a functionary who is just getting on with his job:

'Are you asking for your husband to be committed?'

This time her face turned instantly purple, her eyes glittered, and her lip trembled with rage.

'I don't think I've said anything that would lead you . . .'

The blow had struck home, and she began rising to her feet to bring the conversation to an end.

'Sit down, please. Calm down. I don't see why this very natural question should upset you so much. In short, what did you come to tell me? Don't forget that this is the Police Judiciaire, where we deal with crimes and misdemeanours, either to arrest those responsible or, more rarely, to prevent them from happening. First of all, you told me that for some months your husband has seemed to be afflicted with nervous exhaustion . . .'

'I said . . .'

'You said: nervous exhaustion. And his behaviour worried you so much that you sent him to a neurologist . . .'

'I advised him . . .'

'Let's say that you advised him to consult a neurologist. Did you expect that he would recommend that your husband be committed?'

With her features more pinched and her voice changed, she replied:

'I expected him to treat my husband.'

'Fine. And I assume he did?'

'I have no idea.'

'You called Doctor Steiner, or you went to see him, and he withdrew behind patient confidentiality.'

She was looking at him steadily, her nerves tense, as if to guess what his next attack might be.

'Since his visit to the doctor, has your husband been taking medication?'

'Not that I know of.'

'Has his attitude changed?'

'He still seems just as depressed as before.'

'Depressed, but not agitated?'

'I don't know. I don't see what you're trying to get at.'

'What are you afraid of?'

This time it was she who took her time, wondering where the question was leading.

'Are you asking me if I am afraid of my husband?'

'Yes.'

'I'm afraid *for* him. I'm not afraid *of* him.'

'Why?'

'Because, whatever happens, I'm capable of defending myself.'

'Then let me return to my initial question. Why did you come and see me this afternoon?'

'Because he came to see you this morning.'

The two of them weren't following the same logic. Or perhaps she didn't want to follow the same logic as Maigret.'

'You knew what he was going to say to me?'

'If I had known, I . . .'

She bit her lip. Was she about to say: 'I shouldn't have bothered'?

Maigret didn't have time to think about it, because the phone rang on his desk. He picked it up.

'Hello, chief! Janvier here . . . I'm in the office next door. They told me who you had there, and I preferred not to show my face . . . I'd like to talk to you for a moment . . .'

'I'm coming . . .'

He got to his feet and apologized.

'Will you excuse me? They need me on another matter. I won't be long.'

In the inspectors' office he said to Lucas:

'Go into the corridor, and if she tries to leave as her husband did, hold her back.'

He closed the connecting door again. Torrence had sent for a glass of beer and, mechanically, Maigret drank it with satisfaction.

'Any news?'

'I went over there. You know Avenue de Châtillon. You would almost think you were in the provinces, even though you're not far from Avenue d'Orléans. Number 17, where they live, is a new building, six floors, yellow brick. Most of the tenants are office workers and salespeople.

'You must be able to hear everything from one apartment to the next, and there are children on all the floors.

'The Martons don't live in the building as such. It stands on the site of a town-house which has since been demolished. The courtyard was left, with a tree in the middle and, at the end, a two-storey house.

'An external staircase leads to the first floor, where there are only two bedrooms and a study.

'Eighteen years ago, when Xavier Marton, still a bachelor, first rented this accommodation, the ground floor, with its completely glazed façade, was a carpenter's workshop.

'Then the carpenter left. Marton rented the ground floor and turned it into a pleasant room, half workshop, half living room.

'The overall effect is unexpected, pretty and amusing. It isn't a flat like any other. At first I suggested a life insurance policy to the concierge. She listened to my patter without interrupting me, then told me that she didn't need one because eventually she would have her pension. I asked her about any tenants who might be open to the idea of becoming clients. She told me a number of names.

'"They all pay National Insurance," she added. "You won't have much luck . . ."

'"Don't you have a Monsieur Marton?"

'"At the end of the courtyard, yes . . . Maybe them . . . ? They earn a good living . . . Last year they bought a car . . . Try them . . ."

'"Will I find anyone there?"

'"I think so."

'You see, chief, it wasn't all that difficult. I rang at the workshop door. A young woman opened it.

'"Madame Marton?" I asked.

'"No, my sister won't be back until about seven."'

Maigret had frowned.

'What's the sister like?'

'The sort of woman who turns men's heads in the street. As for me . . .'

'Were you impressed?'

'Hard to describe. I'd say she's thirty-five at most. It's not so much that she's pretty, or dazzling. Neither was I struck by her elegance, because she was wearing a little black linen dress and her hair was untidy – like a woman who's doing her housework. Except . . .'

'Except?'

'It's just that there's something very feminine, very touching about her. She seems very gentle, slightly frightened by life, and that's the kind of woman that a man wants to protect. Do you see what I mean? Her body is also very feminine, very . . .'

He blushed at Maigret's amused smile.

'Did you stay with her for a long time?'

'About ten minutes. I talked about insurance at first. She told me that her brother-in-law and her sister had both signed up for a major insurance policy about a year ago . . .'

'Did she tell you the exact sum?'

'No. I just know that it's with the Mutuelle. She added that she herself didn't need insurance, because she already had a pension. Along one of the walls there is a table, with a complicated electric train, near a workbench. I told her I had just bought a train set for my son. That allowed me to stay for longer. She asked me if I had bought the train set from the Magasins du Louvre, and I said I had.

'"Then it must have been my brother-in-law who served you . . ."'

'Is that all?' Maigret asked him.

'More or less. I saw two or three sales representatives, but I didn't dare to be too specific. The Martons seem to be well regarded in the area, and to pay their rent regularly.'

Maigret suddenly noticed that it was Torrence's glass that he had emptied.

'Sorry, old man. Send another one up on my account . . .'
He added:

'And one for me. I'll come and drink it when I've finished with the woman who came to see me.'

She hadn't moved from her armchair in his absence but had lit a cigarette.

He returned to his place and put his hands flat on the desk.

'I can't remember where we were. Ah yes! You invited me to question you. But I don't really see what I can ask you. Do you have a maid, Madame Marton? Because, if I've understood you correctly, you work all day.'

'All day, yes.'

'For yourself?'

'Not exactly. However, my boss, Monsieur Harris, who set up the lingerie house on Rue Saint-Honoré, gives me quite a high commission, because I'm usually the one who keeps the business going.'

'So you have an important position?'

'Quite important, yes.'

'I think I may have heard of the Harris house.'

'It's one of the three best houses in Paris for fine lingerie. We have a select clientele, including crowned heads.'

This gave him a clearer sense of certain details that had

struck him at the beginning, the discreet and yet slightly particular elegance of his visitor. As happens in certain fashion houses and in certain businesses, she had gradually acquired the tastes and attitudes of her clientele, while at the same time retaining an indispensable modesty.

'Were your parents in lingerie?'

She relaxed, now that they were on more ordinary territory, and the questions seemed innocent.

'Far from it. My father was a history teacher at a school in Rouen, and my mother never did anything in her life apart from being the daughter of a general.'

'Do you have brothers and sisters?'

'One sister, who spent a certain amount of time in the United States, in Green Village, New Jersey, not far from New York, with her husband. Her husband was an engineer in an oil refinery.'

'You say: "was"?'

'He was killed two years ago in an explosion in the laboratories. My sister came back to France, so shaken, so discouraged, that we took her into our house.'

'I asked you just now if you had a maid.'

'No. My sister doesn't work. She has never worked in her life. She is younger than me and she married at the age of twenty, when she was still living with my parents. She has always been a spoilt child.'

'Does she do your housework?'

'It's her way of paying her share, if you like. We didn't ask, she volunteered.'

'Were you also living with your parents when you met your husband?'

'No. Unlike Jenny – she's my sister – I didn't feel Rouen was the place for me and I got on quite badly with my mother. As soon as I graduated from high school I came to Paris.'

'Alone?'

'What do you mean?'

'You had no friends here?'

'I see. Since I'm the one who invited you to question me, I have no excuse not to answer you. I came to find someone I knew, in fact, a young lawyer, and we lived together for a few months. It didn't work, and I looked for a job. Then I realized that my high-school certificate, by which my father set such store that he tortured me for years, is useless. All I could find, after weeks of toing and froing around Paris, was a job as a saleswoman at the Magasins du Louvre.'

'And you met Marton.'

'Not straight away. We weren't on the same floor. We finally became acquainted on the Métro.'

'Was he already the head salesman?'

'Certainly not.'

'Are you married?'

'That's what he wanted. I would have been happy to live with him . . .'

'Do you love him?'

'Why would I be here otherwise?'

'When did you leave the shop?'

'Wait . . . About . . . It'll be five years ago next month.'

'So after seven years of marriage.'

'More or less.'

'And at that point your husband had become head of department?'

'Yes.'

'But you were still a humble salesgirl.'

'I don't see what you're getting at.'

He said, thoughtfully:

'Neither do I. So you went to work for Monsieur Harris.'

'That's not exactly how it happened. First of all, Harris is the name of the company. My boss's real name is Maurice Schwob. He worked at the Magasins du Louvre, where he was lingerie buyer.'

'How old?'

'Now?'

'Yes.'

'Forty-nine. But it's not what you think. Our relationship is purely businesslike. He has always planned to branch out on his own. In his shop he needed a young woman who knew the trade. When it comes to lingerie and girdles, women don't like being served by a man. He had noticed me at the Louvre. That's the whole story.'

'Are you effectively partners?'

'In a sense, although my interests in the business are much smaller than his, which is perfectly natural, since he put up the original funds and he does the designs.'

'In short, until about five years ago your husband's position was more important than yours. And he had a larger salary. But for five years the opposite has been the case. Is that right?'

'That's right, but believe me, it's not something I even think about.'

'And your husband doesn't either?'

She hesitated.

'At first men aren't keen for that to happen. He's got used to it. We still live modestly.'

'Do you have a car?'

'Yes, we do, but we barely use it except at the weekend and on holiday.'

'Do you go on holiday with your sister?'

'Why not?'

'Why not, indeed?'

There was quite a long silence. Maigret looked embarrassed.

'I can't think of any more questions to ask you. Tell me, Madame Marton, what would you like me to do?'

That was enough to put her on the defensive again.

'I still don't understand,' she murmured.

'You don't want us to keep an eye on your husband?'

'Why would you do that?'

'Are you willing to sign a formal request which would allow us to make him undergo a medical examination?'

'Certainly not.'

'So that's everything?'

'That's everything . . . I suppose . . .'

'In that case I don't see any reason to keep you here any longer.'

He got to his feet. She did the same, a little stiffly. As he led her towards the door he seemed to change his mind.

'Do you use zinc phosphide?'

She didn't give a start. She must have been waiting for

that question all along, and perhaps she had even come here just to answer it.

'I do use it, yes.'

'For what purpose?'

'Rue Saint-Honoré is one of the oldest streets in Paris and, behind the luxury boutiques, most of the houses are in a bad state; there is a whole network of courtyards, alleys and passageways that you wouldn't even guess were there. And the proximity of the market also attracts an extraordinary number of rats, and they have damaged the merchandise. We tried several products without success. Someone recommended to Monsieur Schwob that he use zinc phosphide, which gave excellent results.

'And we had rats on Avenue de Châtillon as well, and my husband complained about them. I took a certain amount of phosphide from the shop . . .'

'Without mentioning it to your husband?'

'I can't remember whether I talked to him about it or not.'

She stared wide-eyed, as if an idea had struck her.

'I don't suppose he imagined . . . ?'

He didn't finish the sentence for her and she went on:

'If he talked to you about it, it's because . . . My God! And there I was racking my brains to guess what was troubling him . . . I'll sort things out with him this evening . . . Then again . . . If I broach that subject he'll know I've come to see you . . .'

'Did you think you'd be able to hide it from him?'

'I don't know, I don't know any more, Monsieur Maigret. I came . . . how should I put it . . . ? I came candidly, with the idea – a naive one, in fact – of confiding in you. I have told you the truth about Xavier and about my anxieties. Rather than helping me, you asked me questions which, I realize, indicate that you don't believe me, that you suspect me of planning heaven knows what . . .'

She wasn't crying but did seem to be in a certain amount of distress.

'Too bad . . . ! I had hoped . . . I have no option but to do my best . . .'

She opened the door with her gloved hand. Standing in the corridor, she said again:

'Goodbye, inspector . . . And thank you for seeing me anyway . . .'

Maigret watched her walk away with short, precise steps, perched on very high heels, and shrugged as he went back into his office. A quarter of an hour had passed by the time he left and went to the chief's office, asking Joseph in passing:

'Is the commissioner in?'

'No. He's in a meeting with the prefect and he told me he probably wouldn't be back before this afternoon.'

Maigret still went into the office of the commissioner of the Police Judiciaire, turned on the lamp and started reading the titles of the books that filled the two mahogany bookshelves. There were works on statistics that no one had ever opened, technical books in several languages that the publishers sent as a matter of course. There were many criminology textbooks, and works on forensics and legal medicine.

At last, on a shelf, Maigret saw several books on

psychiatry, and flicked through three or four before choosing one which seemed to be written in a simpler and more accessible language than the others.

That evening he took the book home. After dinner, in slippers in front of the log fire, with the radio turned down, he began to read while Madame Maigret repaired the cuffs of some shirts.

He didn't plan to read the whole of the thick book, and there were whole pages which, in spite of his brief medical studies, he was unable to understand.

He looked for certain chapter headings, certain words that had come up that morning during his conversation with Pardon, words whose meaning everyone thinks they know, but which have a very different resonance for professionals.

. . . Neuroses . . . For Adler, the source of the neuroses is a threatening feeling of inferiority and insecurity . . . A defensive reaction against the patient's feeling drives the patient to identify with a fictional ideal structure . . .

He repeated it under his breath, making his wife look up:
'. . . fictional ideal structure . . .'

. . . Physical syndrome . . . Neurasthenics are well known to specialists of all kinds . . . Without any appreciable damage to the organs, they suffer and, more particularly, worry about possible complications; they have multiple consultations and examinations . . .

. . . Mental syndrome . . . The feeling of incapacity is dominant . . . Physically, the patient feels lethargic and in pain, tired by the slightest effort . . .

Like Maigret that very morning. Now he still felt lethargic, perhaps not in pain, but . . .

He sullenly turned the pages.

. . . A constitution that is said to be paranoid . . . Hypertrophy of the Ego . . .

. . . Unlike hypersensitive individuals, these patients project on to family and particularly on to social life an inflated and dominant Ego . . .

. . . They never see themselves as being at fault or responsible for anything . . . They are characterized by a strong sense of pride . . . Even if they are relatively unintelligent, they often dominate their families with their authoritarianism and their trenchant certainty . . .

Was it Xavier Marton that this applied to, or his wife? And couldn't it be applied to a quarter of the population of Paris?

Vindictive psychosis . . . Persecuted-persecuting . . .

. . . This is a typical passionate psychosis the nosological situation of which has led to interminable discussions . . . With Kraepelin and Capgras, I contend that it does not fall among the class of true deliria . . . The patient considers himself the victim of an injustice which he wants to put right and attempts to obtain satisfaction regardless of the cost . . .

Xavier Marton? Madame Marton?

He moved from neuroses to psychoses, from psychoses to psychoneuroses, from hysteria to paranoia and, like those people who immerse themselves in a medical dictionary and discover that they are suffering from every illness in turn, under each heading he found symptoms that would apply equally well to one or other of his characters.

From time to time he grunted, repeated a word or a phrase, and Madame Maigret darted him anxious little glances.

In the end he got up, as a man who has had enough, threw the book on the table and, opening the sideboard in the dining room, picked up the bottle of plum brandy and filled one of the little gold-rimmed glasses.

It was like a protestation of common sense against all that scientific gobbledygook, a way of getting back down to earth.

Pardon was right: by investigating the anomalies of human behaviour, classifying and subdividing them, in the end it was impossible to tell what a man of sound mind might be.

Was he even one himself? From what he had just read, he was no longer so sure.

'Do you have a difficult case on?' Madame Maigret asked shyly; she seldom inquired into her husband's activities at Quai des Orfèvres.

He merely shrugged and grumbled:

'Just some mad people!'

He added a little later, after draining his glass:

'Let's go to bed.'

But the next morning he asked to see the commissioner a few minutes before the morning briefing, and the chief saw immediately that he was troubled.

'What's wrong, Maigret?'

He tried to tell him the story of the two visits as succinctly as possible. His boss's first reaction was to look at him with a degree of surprise.

'I don't see what's bothering you. Since we haven't received a formal complaint . . .'

'That's it exactly. Each of them came to tell me their little story. And neither story, in itself, is a cause for concern. But when you try to compare the two, you notice that they don't match . . . In fact, let me give you back your book . . .'

He set it down on the desk, and the commissioner looked at the title, then looked at the inspector with even greater surprise.

'Listen to what I'm saying, chief. And don't imagine that I've been hoodwinked by this book. I'm not claiming that either of the two is entirely mad. But there's still something that isn't quite right. There must be a reason why two people, husband and wife, come to see me on the same day as if delivering a confession. If, tomorrow or in a week, or in a month, we learned that there was a corpse, my conscience wouldn't be clear . . .'

'Is that what you think?'

'I don't know. I'm in two minds. It's a little like carrying out an investigation in reverse. Usually we have a crime at the beginning, and it's only once it's been committed that we try and find the motives for it. This time we have motives but as yet no crime.'

'Don't you think there might be thousands of cases when motives aren't followed by a crime?'

'I'm sure. Except in those cases no one came to present them to me *beforehand*.'

His boss thought for a moment.

'I'm starting to understand.'

'Where we are at the moment, there's nothing I can do. Particularly after the recent press coverage of the police taking liberties with suspects.'

'So?'

'I came to ask your permission to talk to the public prosecutor just in case.'

'So that he can order an investigation?'

'More or less. To put my conscience at rest, in any case.'

'I doubt it will work.'

'Me too.'

'Well, if it makes you feel better.'

'Thank you, chief.'

He hadn't said exactly what he had promised himself he would say, perhaps because the matter was too complicated and still confused. At this time the previous day he had never heard of the Martons; now the train-set specialist was beginning to haunt his thoughts, as was the elegant young woman who, he admitted, had boldly stood up to him when he had done everything he could to unsettle her.

Even the widowed sister-in-law, a poignant woman according to Janvier, worried him as if he had known her for ever.

'Hello! Maigret here. Would you ask the public prosecutor if he could grant me a few minutes . . . ? This morning if possible, yes . . . Hello! I'll stay on the line . . .'

It was in the Palais de Justice too, in the same building but in a different world, where the walls were covered in carved wooden panels and where people talked in low voices.

'Straight away . . . ? Yes . . . I'm on my way . . .'

He passed through the glass-panelled door separating the two universes, walked past some lawyers in black gowns and, as he waited between two gendarmes near anonymous doors, he spotted people who had passed through his hands several weeks or several months earlier. Some of them seemed happy to see him again and greeted him almost as if he was an old friend.

'If you would be so kind as to wait for a moment, the public prosecutor will see you presently . . .'

It was almost as impressive as being allowed into the headmaster's office at school.

'Come in, Maigret. You asked to see me? But nothing new has happened . . . ?'

'I would like to submit a case that is almost a case of conscience . . .'

He gave a very bad account of the story, even worse

than the one he had given to the commissioner of the Police Judiciaire.

'If I understand you correctly, you have a sense that an incident is about to happen, perhaps a crime?'

'That's more or less it.'

'But this impression is not based on anything precise, only the vague confidences of a man and the explanations that his wife then spontaneously gave you? Tell me, Maigret, how many lunatics, cranks, maniacs and plain eccentrics do you welcome into your office every year?'

'Hundreds . . .'

'And in here I receive thousands of letters from the same people.'

The prosecutor looked at him in silence, as if he had said all there was to say.

'I would still have liked to make an investigation,' Maigret murmured shyly.

'What kind of investigation? Let's be precise. Questioning the neighbours, the employers, the sister-in-law, the suppliers, and so forth? First of all, I don't see where that will get you. Then, if the Martons are awkward customers, they would be perfectly within their rights to complain . . .'

'I know . . .'

'As to obliging them both to undergo psychiatric examination, that is not possible while no formal request has been submitted to us by either party. And in any case . . . !'

'And if a crime is committed . . . ?'

A brief silence. A slight shrug.

'That would be regrettable, certainly, but there would

be nothing we could do about it. And at the very least, in that case, we wouldn't have far to look to find the guilty party.'

'But will you allow me to keep them under surveillance?'

'On condition, first of all, that it is done discreetly enough not to cause us any difficulties. And secondly, that it does not mean using inspectors who would be more useful elsewhere . . .'

'We are in a period of dead calm . . .'

'Those periods never last long. If you want to know what I really think, you are being over-scrupulous. If I were you, Maigret, I would drop the case. Once again, as things stand, we have no right to intervene, and no way of doing so. These husbands and wives suspecting one another – I'm sure there are thousands of them all around us . . .'

'But neither the husband nor the wife has come to me for help.'

'They really asked for your help?'

He had to agree that they hadn't. Marton definitely hadn't asked for anything. Neither had Madame Marton. And the sister, Jenny, certainly hadn't.

'I'm sorry you can't stay. Five or six people are waiting for me, and I have a meeting at the Ministry at eleven o'clock.'

'I'm sorry for disturbing you.'

Maigret wasn't happy with himself. He had a sense that he had argued his case badly. Perhaps he shouldn't have immersed himself in that psychiatric textbook the previous evening.

He walked towards the door. The public prosecutor called him back at the last minute, and his tone was no longer the same: his voice was suddenly as cold as if he had been delivering one of his famous summings-up.

'It is understood, of course, that I will not cover for you and that I have forbidden you to pursue this case until a new development occurs.'

'Understood, sir.'

And in the corridor he grumbled, with his head lowered:

'. . . new development . . . new development . . .'

Who would be the *new development*, meaning the victim? Him or her?

He slammed the door so abruptly that he nearly shattered the glass.

4. The Restaurant on Rue Coquillière

It wasn't the first time, and it probably wouldn't be the last, that Maigret flew into a rage as he left the public prosecutor's office, and his disputes with certain judges, with Examining Magistrate Coméliau in particular, who had been something like his friendly enemy for over twenty years, were legendary at Quai des Orfèvres.

When he had a clear head, he wasn't too troubled by the antagonism that existed between the two worlds. On either side of the glass door, each of them, more or less, got on conscientiously with their job. The same people, low-lifes, criminals, suspects and witnesses, passed through their hands one by one.

The main difference, the one which created tacit conflicts, was the perspective one assumed. Did that perspective not flow directly from the way that both sides were recruited? The people in the public prosecutor's office – prosecutors, deputy prosecutors, examining magistrates – almost all of them belonged to the middle, if not the upper strata of the bourgeoisie. Their lifestyle, after purely theoretical studies, barely brought them into contact, except in their practice, with the people they were meant to pursue in the name of society.

Hence their almost congenital lack of understanding of certain problems, an irritating attitude in the face of certain cases which the men of the Police Judiciaire, who lived, so to speak, in permanent and almost physical intimacy with the criminal world, assessed instinctively.

There was also a tendency on the part of the Palais de Justice to be a little hypocritical. In spite of an apparent much-discussed independence, they were more susceptible than most to a ministerial frown, and if a case that had stirred public opinion dragged a little, they hounded the police, who could never move quickly enough. It was up to the police to come up with a strategy and use the appropriate methods.

But if the newspapers criticized those methods, the magistrates of the public prosecutor's office would hurry to take them to task.

Not without reason had the inspector gone to see the public prosecutor. As regularly happens, they were in a difficult situation at the moment. An incident had occurred, luckily not the fault of the Police Judiciaire, but of the Sûreté Générale in Rue des Saussaies, which had degenerated, leading to questions in parliament.

In a nightclub, the son of a parliamentary deputy had violently struck an inspector who, he claimed, had been tailing him for several days. A general punch-up had ensued. It had been impossible to hush up the case, and the Sûreté had been obliged to admit that they were investigating the young suspect not only for heroin use, but for procuring new clients for the dealers.

All kinds of revolting things had come to light as a result. According to the deputy whose son had been struck, one of the dealers was a police informer, and his father claimed that the order to turn his son into a drug addict had been deliberately issued by the Ministry of the Interior in order to compromise him as a politician.

So for a while the police had a bad press, and that morning Maigret had preferred to take his precautions.

Back in his office, he was still determined to bypass the instructions he had been given, not least because those instructions are never meant to be taken literally. The prosecutor had been covering his own back, quite simply, and if a corpse was found on Avenue de Châtillon tomorrow, he would be the first to rebuke the inspector for his inaction.

Since he had to cheat, he cheated, but without enthusiasm. He could no longer use Janvier, whom, curiously enough, Marton had spotted straight away at the Magasins du Louvre, and who had already paid a visit to the Marton household.

Of all the others, it was Lucas who would have shown the greatest flair and deftness, but Lucas had one flaw: it was easy to guess his profession.

He chose young Lapointe, who was less well trained, less experienced, but who could often pass for a student or a young clerk.

'Listen, son . . .'

He gave him a long, slow briefing, so detailed that his instructions actually became quite unclear. First he was to go and buy some kind of toy, without hanging about, without making a fuss, at the Magasins du Louvre, with a view to spotting Marton and recognizing him again in future.

Then, at lunchtime, he was to stay near the staff door and follow the train-set specialist.

He was to start again in the evening, if necessary. Meanwhile, that afternoon, he was to take a look at the lingerie boutique on Rue Saint-Honoré.

'There's no reason to suspect that you're not engaged . . .'

Lapointe blushed, because it was almost the case. Only almost, because the engagement was not yet official.

'You could, for example, buy a nightdress for your fiancée. Ideally not something too expensive . . .'

And Lapointe replied shyly:

'Do you think you give your fiancée a nightie as a present? Isn't that a bit intimate?'

Afterwards they would see how they might find out more, without revealing themselves, about the Martons and their young sister-in-law.

Once Lapointe had left, Maigret went back to work, signing documents and mail, listening to the reports of his inspectors about unimportant matters. Marton and his wife were always there, like a backdrop, behind the concerns of the moment.

There was a faint hope that he didn't really believe in: that they would come and tell him that Xavier Marton was asking to see him.

Why not? When he had left the previous day while Maigret was with his boss, was it not because the time he had allocated himself had passed, because he had to get back to the shop before a certain time? In such establishments, discipline is very strict. Maigret was well aware of this, not least because when he started out he had spent almost two years policing the big department stores. He knew the atmosphere, the intricacies, the rules and intrigues.

At midday, he came back to Boulevard Richard-Lenoir for lunch and noticed at last that it was grilled meat for the third day in a row. He remembered in time his wife's visit to Pardon. She must have expected him to be surprised by the new menus and she had probably prepared a more or less plausible explanation.

He avoided putting her in that situation and was gentle with her, perhaps slightly too much so, because she was looking at him with a hint of anxiety.

Of course, he wasn't thinking about the trio on Avenue de Châtillon all the time. The subject only came to mind every now and again, in little bursts, almost unconsciously.

It was a little like a puzzle, and it irritated him, like a jigsaw that you keep coming back to in spite of yourself, to put a piece in place. The difference being that in this instance the pieces were human beings.

Had he been hard on Gisèle Marton, whose lip had been trembling when she left him, as if she was about to cry?

It was possible. He hadn't done it on purpose. His job was to try and find things out. Basically he found her quite sympathetic, like her husband. He was sympathetic with couples, and disappointed every time a misunderstanding appeared between a man and a woman who had once loved each other.

They must have loved each other, when they worked together at the Magasins du Louvre, when they only had two uncomfortable rooms above the workshop.

Little by little they had improved their apartment. Once the carpenter had left, they had expanded by renting the ground floor, which, according to Janvier, had become a nice room, and had had an interior staircase built so that they didn't have to go outside to move from one floor to the other.

Now they were both what one would call well-to-do, and they had bought a car.

There was a flaw, that much was obvious. But what was it?

An idea ran through his head, and it would return to him several times. He was troubled by Marton's visit to Doctor Steiner, because throughout his career he couldn't remember a man going to a neurologist or a psychiatrist to ask him: 'Do you think I'm mad?'

His idea was that perhaps Marton had read, whether by chance or otherwise, a psychiatric textbook of the kind that the inspector had flicked through the previous evening.

While he was mulling over the people on Avenue de Châtillon, Maigret went on answering phone calls. He spoke to a shopkeeper reporting a theft from her window display, whom he sent to her local inspector, and paced about in the inspectors' office, which was still dead calm.

Lapointe gave no sign of life, and at about five o'clock Maigret found himself back in his office, lining up words in a column on the yellow jacket of a file.

First of all he had written: *frustration.*

Then, below it: *inferiority complex.*

Those were terms that he didn't normally use, and which he mistrusted. A few years previously he had had an inspector who was just out of university and who had been with the Police Judiciaire for only a few months. He probably worked for a legal firm now. He had read Freud, Adler and a few others and had been so influenced by them that he claimed to be able to explain any case that came in with reference to psychoanalysis.

During his brief stay at the Police Judiciaire he had made one mistake after the other, and his colleagues had nicknamed him Inspector Complex.

The case of Xavier Marton was no less curious, in that he seemed to have sprung fully formed from the pages of the book that Maigret had read the previous evening, and which he had ended up slamming impatiently shut.

Whole pages of the book dealt with frustration and its consequences on the behaviour of the individual. It included examples that might have been a portrait of Marton.

A child who had grown up in care, he had spent his childhood on a poor farm in the Sologne, with harsh and brutal farmers who tore the books out of his hands when they caught him reading.

Still, he had devoured all the printed pages that he had been able to lay his hands on at random: popular novels, scientific works, mechanics manuals, poems, gulping down the good and the bad indifferently.

He had taken his first step in joining a department store, where, at first, he had been entrusted with only the humblest of tasks.

One fact was typical. As soon as Marton had the chance, he stopped living in more or less moth-eaten furnished rooms, like most people starting out in Paris, and had instead had his own flat. It was only two rooms at the end of a courtyard; the furnishing was basic, comfort non-existent, but it was his.

He rose through the ranks. He already had the illusion of a regular, bourgeois existence, and his first concern was to improve the interior with the scant means at his disposal.

That was what Maigret put under the heading: inferiority complex. More precisely, it was Marton's reaction to that complex.

The man needed to reassure himself. He also needed to show other people that he was not an inferior being, and he worked hard to become an uncontested expert in his specialization.

In his mind, did he not consider himself as something like the Train-Set King?

He was becoming someone. He had become someone. And, when he married, it was to a girl of a middle-class background, the daughter of a schoolteacher, who had passed her school-leaving exam, whose manners were different from those of the little salesgirls that surrounded her.

Maigret tentatively wrote down a third word: *humiliation*.

Marton's wife had overtaken him. She was now almost independent, working in a luxury business where every day she met notable women, high society, *le Tout-Paris*. She earned more than he did.

Certain phrases stayed with Maigret from what he had read the previous day. He couldn't remember them literally, but in spite of himself he tried to apply them to his problem.

One, for example, saying essentially that 'psychopaths close themselves away in a world of their own, a world of dreams which is more important to them than reality'. It wasn't that exactly, but he wasn't going to make himself look ridiculous by going to his chief's office and consulting the book again.

And besides, he didn't believe it. It was all airy speculation.

Did the train sets not only on Rue de Rivoli, but in the workshop on Avenue de Châtillon not correspond reasonably well to that 'dream world', that 'closed world'.

Another passage reminded him of the calm of Xavier Marton, the conversation at Quai des Orfèvres, the apparently clear way in which he had argued his case.

Maigret could no longer remember whether it fell under the heading of neuroses, psychoses or paranoia, because the boundaries between those different domains didn't strike him as very clear.

. . . starting from false premises . . .

No. It wasn't quite that.

. . . on false or imaginary premises, the patient constructs a rigorous reasoning that is sometimes subtle and brilliant . . .

There was something similar about persecution, but here 'the persecuted individual starts off from real facts and draws conclusions which have the appearance of logic'.

The zinc phosphide was real. And in the partnership of Harris/Gisèle Marton, or rather Maurice Schwob/Gisèle Marton, was there not a certain ambiguity that might affect the husband?

The most worrying thing in this case was that, looking at it in close up, the young woman's behaviour, studied in the light of the same texts, led to an almost identical diagnosis.

She too was intelligent. She too described their case with evident clarity. She too . . .

To hell with it all!

Maigret looked for an eraser to rub out the words he had written on the yellow file, filled a pipe and went and stood by the window, outside of which, in the darkness, he could see nothing but the dots of the streetlights.

By the time young Lapointe knocked at his door half an hour later, he was dutifully filling in the blanks of an administrative questionnaire.

Lapointe had the advantage of coming from outside, from real life, and there was still a bit of chilly air in the folds of his overcoat, his nose was pink with cold, and he was rubbing his hands together to warm them up.

'I did what you told me, chief . . .'

'Wasn't he suspicious?'

'I don't think he noticed me.'

'Tell me.'

'First of all I went up to the toy department and bought

the cheapest toy I could find, a little car that isn't even clockwork . . .'

He took it from his pocket and set it down on the desk. It was canary yellow.

'One hundred and ten francs. I immediately recognized Marton from your description, but it was a salesgirl who served me. Then, waiting for midday, I went and took a glance at Rue Saint-Honoré, without going in. The shop isn't far from Place Vendôme. A narrow shop window with hardly anything in it: a dressing gown, a black silk slip and a pair of gold-edged satin mules. On the glass, two words: *Harris, lingerie*. Inside it's more like a drawing room than a shop, and you can tell that it's a luxury establishment.'

'Did you see her?'

'Yes. I'll come to that in a moment. It was time for me to go back to the Louvre, where I waited near the staff door. At midday it's a real crush, like at the end of school, and everyone hurries to nearby restaurants. Marton came out, in even more of a hurry than the others, and started walking very quickly along Rue du Louvre. He kept looking all around him, and turned round two or three times without paying me any attention. At that time of day there is a lot of traffic, and the pavements are crammed . . .

'He turned left into Rue Coquillière, where he walked only about a hundred metres before going into a little restaurant called Le Trou Normand. The façade is painted brown, with yellow letters, and a printed menu hangs on the left-hand side of the door.

'I hesitated and then decided to go inside a few moments

after him. It was full. You could see that the people were regulars, and on one wall there is a box where the customers keep their napkins. I stopped at the bar. I had a drink.

'"Any chance of lunch?"

'The manager, in a blue apron, looked around the room, where there are only about ten tables.

'"There will be a table free in a few minutes. Table number three is on the cheese course."

'Marton was sitting at the back, near the kitchen door, alone with a paper napkin and a set of cutlery. There was an empty chair opposite him. He said something to one of the two waitresses, who seemed to know him, and she brought him a second set of cutlery.

'A few minutes passed. Marton, who had unfolded a newspaper, kept looking over the top of it in the direction of the door.

'Soon, in fact, a woman came in, immediately spotted the table at the back and went and sat on the free chair as if she was used to it. They didn't kiss, they didn't shake hands. They merely smiled at each other, and it seemed to me that their smile was a little sad, or at the very least a little melancholy.'

'Was it his wife?' Maigret interrupted.

'No, I had just seen his wife on Rue Saint-Honoré and I'll talk to you about that again. From what you've told me, it was the sister-in-law. The age and appearance are a perfect match. I don't know how to explain it . . .'

The truly surprising thing was that Janvier had used almost exactly the same words to describe her.

'You might say that she's a real woman, I don't know if you understand what I mean by that, the kind of woman who is made to love a man. Not to love him in an ordinary way, but the way all men dream of being loved . . .'

Maigret couldn't help smiling at the sight of Lapointe blushing.

'I thought you were almost engaged?'

'I'm trying to explain the effect that she must have on most people. Sometimes you meet a woman like that who immediately makes you think of . . .'

He couldn't find the words.

'Of what?'

'In spite of yourself you see her nestling against her companion's arm, you can almost feel her warmth . . . at the same time you know that she is meant for one man alone, that she is truly in love, a genuine lover . . . I soon found a seat two tables away from them, and that impression stayed with me throughout the whole meal . . . There wasn't the slightest ambiguous gesture . . . They didn't hold hands . . . I don't think they even looked one another in the eyes . . . And yet . . .'

'You think they love each other?'

'I don't think so. I'm sure of it. Even the waitress in the black dress and the white apron, a tall, thin woman with unkempt hair, didn't serve them the way she served everyone else, and she looked as if she was acting as their accomplice . . .'

'And yet you said at the beginning that they were sad.'

'Let's say serious . . . I don't know, chief . . . I'm sure

they aren't miserable, because you can't be truly unhappy when you're . . .'

Maigret smiled again as he wondered what sort of report he might have had from Lucas, for example, who certainly wouldn't have had the same reaction as young Lapointe.

'Not unhappy, but sad, then, like lovers who aren't free to show their love . . .'

'If you like. At one point he got up to take off her coat, because she had glanced at the fire. It was a black woollen coat with a bit of fur around the collar and the wrists. She was also wearing a black jersey dress, and I was surprised to see that she was almost plump . . .

'He consulted his watch several times. Then he asked the waitress to bring him his dessert and coffee, while his companion was still on her joint of veal.

'He got up while she was still eating, and by way of goodbye he rested his hand on her shoulder, with a gesture that was both simple and tender.

'He turned around in the doorway and fluttered his eyelashes . . .

'I don't know if I was right to stay. I told myself that he was going back to the shop. I finished my lunch at almost the same time as the woman did. Marton had paid the bill before leaving. I paid mine. I left behind her and, without hurrying, she went and caught the bus to Porte d'Orléans. I imagined that she was going back to Avenue de Châtillon and didn't follow her. Did I do wrong?'

'You did well. And then?'

'I went for a short walk before going back to Rue

Saint-Honoré, because few luxury boutiques open before two o'clock, some not before half past two. I didn't want to get there too early. I should also confess that I was slightly nervous. And I wanted to see the boss, and told myself that he was probably the kind of man who has lunch in posh restaurants and is in no great hurry.'

Maigret looked at Lapointe with slightly paternal benevolence, because he had taken him under his wing two years earlier, when the young man had come to Quai des Orfèvres, and he had made surprising progress.

'I'm going to confess something to you, chief. I was so scared at the thought of going into a shop like that that I treated myself to a calvados first.'

'Go on.'

'I was about to make my first entrance through the glass door when I noticed two old ladies in mink coats sitting opposite the saleswoman, and I didn't dare. I waited for them to leave. A chauffeur-driven Rolls was waiting for them a little way off.

'Then, for fear that a new customer might arrive, I hurried up.

'At first I didn't look at anything around me, I was so scared.

'"I would like a nightdress for a girl . . ." I recited.

'I assumed it was Madame Marton who was standing in front of me. Besides, when I observed her a little later I saw that she had certain features in common with the young woman in the Trou Normand. Madame Marton is slightly taller, she has a good figure as well, but her body looks harder, what one might call a sculptural body. Do you see what I mean?

'"What kind of nightdress?" she asked me. "Take a seat . . ."

'Because it isn't the kind of shop where you stay standing up. I told you it was like a drawing room. At the back, some curtains hide little compartments that must be changing rooms, and in one of them I saw a big mirror and a wicker stool.

'"What size is the young woman?"

'"She's a bit smaller than you, her shoulders are narrower . . ."

'I don't think she suspected anything, she kept giving me a protective look, and I could sense that she was saying to herself that I must have come to the wrong shop.

'"We have this, in natural silk, with real lace. I imagine it's a gift?"

'I stammered that it was.

'"This is the model that we created for the trousseau of Princess Helena of Greece."

'I wanted to stay for as long as possible. I said, hesitantly:

'"I imagine it's very expensive?"

'"Forty-five thousand . . . It's a size 40 . . . If the girl is a different size, we would have to make the slip to measure because this is all we have in store . . ."

'"You don't have anything less luxurious? Nylon, for example . . . ?"'

Maigret observed:

'Goodness, Lapointe, you seem to know your way

around these things. I thought it wasn't the done thing to buy lingerie for your fiancée . . .'

'I had to play the game. At the word "nylon" she assumed a disdainful, pinched expression.

'"We don't have nylon here. Only natural silk and batiste . . ."

'The door opened. In the mirror, first of all, I saw a man wearing a camel-hair coat, to whom the saleswoman winked, and I'm sure, chief, that her wink meant that she was dealing with an odd customer.

'The man took off his overcoat and hat, walked around the counter and, drawing a silk curtain, went into a cramped little office, where he hung his clothes on the clothes stand. He left a trace of scent in his wake. I went on watching him, leaning over his papers, which he glanced at carelessly.

'Then he came back into the shop, where he looked at his fingernails, then at each of us in turn, like someone in his own home, and seemed to be waiting for me to make my mind up.

'I asked off the top of my head:

'"Do you have it in white? I would like a very simple slip, without lace . . ."

'They exchanged another glance, and the woman bent down to take a cardboard box from a drawer.

'Monsieur Harris, or Schwob, is the kind of man you see a lot around Place Vendôme and the Champs-Élysées, and he could just as easily work in films or exports, paintings or antiques. You know what I mean, don't you? He must spend every morning at his hairdresser's and getting a facial massage. His suit is marvellously well cut, without a crease, and I'm sure he doesn't buy his shoes ready-made.

'He has black hair, a little silver at the temples, and olive skin. He's close-shaven, and looks at you in a haughty, ironic way.

'"This is the cheapest thing we have . . ."

'A slip that looked like nothing at all, with only a couple of bits of embroidery.

'"How much?"

'"Eighteen thousand."

'Another glance between the two of them.

'"I don't suppose this is what you were looking for?"

'And already she was opening the box to put the slip back in.

'"I need to think . . . I'll come back . . ."

'"Of course . . ."

'I almost forgot my hat on the counter and had to go back. Once I was outside and the door was closed, I turned around and saw them both laughing.

'I walked about a hundred metres, then crossed to the opposite pavement. There was no one in the shop. The curtain of the little office was open, the woman was sitting down, and Harris was combing his hair at a mirror . . .

'That's all, chief. I can't swear that they're sleeping together. What is certain is that they make a good couple, and they don't need to speak to understand each other. You can sense that straight away.

'Madame Marton doesn't have lunch with her husband, even though they work five hundred metres apart, and it was her sister-in-law who joined Xavier Marton.

'I suppose, in the end, that those two must be hiding. Marton, in fact, doesn't get much time for lunch. Very close to the Magasins du Louvre there are a number of cheap restaurants which I've seen the sales staff hurrying towards.

'And yet he takes the trouble to go quite a distance, to a bistro with a different clientele, where no one would think of going to look for them.

'Does Madame Marton usually have lunch with Monsieur Harris? I don't know. The fact that he reached the shop after her doesn't prove anything . . .'

Maigret got up to adjust the radiator, which, like the previous day, was tending to overheat. All day they had been expecting snow, which was forecast; the north and Normandy were already covered.

Had Maigret not been right to dismiss the psychiatric textbooks and all those things about psychoses and complexes?

He felt, finally, that he was dealing with people of flesh and blood, men and women with passions and interests.

Yesterday there had merely been one couple.

Today there seemed to be two, and that made an enormous difference.

'Where are you sending me now?' asked Lapointe, who was excited about the case as well and feared being shut out of it.

'You can't go to Rue Saint-Honoré or to Avenue de Châtillon now that the two women have seen you . . .'

And besides, what would he have gone there to do? The public prosecutor seemed to be right. Nothing had happened. Probably nothing would happen. Unless one of the two couples, in the grip of impatience . . .

When the phone rang, Maigret was looking at the time on the black marble clock on the mantelpiece, which was always ten minutes fast. It said it was 5.50.

'Inspector Maigret here . . .'

Why did he feel a faint shock at the sound of the voice? Was it because, since the previous morning, he had been thinking about nothing else than the man at the other end of the line?

There were noises, voices in the background. Maigret could have sworn that the man was anxiously holding his hand cupped over his mouth. He was speaking in a low voice.

'I'm sorry about yesterday, but I had to leave. I just want to know if you will still be at your office about a quarter to seven, perhaps ten to seven. We close at six thirty . . .'

'Today?'

'If you would be so kind . . .'

'I'll wait for you.'

Marton hung up straight away, after stammering a thank you, and Maigret looked at Lapointe rather as Madame Marton and Monsieur Harris had looked at each other in the lingerie boutique.

'Was that him?'

'Yes.'

'Is he on his way?'

'In an hour and a quarter.'

Maigret wanted to make fun of himself, of all the notions he had cooked up about this matter which, an hour and a quarter from now, would probably turn out to have a perfectly simple explanation.

'We have time to go and have a beer at the Brasserie Dauphine,' he growled, opening his cupboard to take out his overcoat and hat.

5. A Woman on the Embankment

It was just as he was about to go downstairs with Lapointe that the idea came to Maigret.

'I'll be with you straight away. Wait for me.'

And, still hesitating, he walked towards the inspectors' office. His idea was that one of his men should follow Xavier Marton when he left the Magasins du Louvre. He didn't know exactly why. Or rather, there were several things that might happen. First of all, Marton was liable to change at the last moment, as he had done once before, leaving Maigret's office when the inspector was elsewhere. And his wife, who confessed to having followed him over the previous few days, was capable of spying on him once more.

If she approached him in the street, wouldn't he follow her to Avenue de Châtillon? There were other possibilities. And even if nothing happened, Maigret was curious to know how the train-set salesman behaved when taking an important step, whether he would hesitate, whether he would stop on the way, for example, to boost his courage with a glass or two.

Janvier risked being recognized. Another inspector acting on his own, Lucas, for example, who was available, but who had never seen Marton, might not be able to spot him, even on the basis of his description, in the crowd of staff leaving the store.

'Lucas and Janvier! Both of you go to the Magasins du Louvre. When the workers leave, Janvier isn't to show himself, just point to Marton in passing, and then Lucas is to follow him on his own.'

Lucas, who didn't really understand what was happening, asked:

'Do you think it'll take a long time, that he'll go far?'

'Here, probably.'

He nearly added:

'But no taxis, no expenses!'

Because there are administrative rules that the public doesn't know but which are sometimes very important for the people in the Police Judiciaire. When a crime or an offence is committed and when the police are delegated by the legal authorities to carry out an investigation the professional expenses of the chief inspectors, inspectors and technicians are in principle the responsibility of the guilty party. If he is not arrested, or if the court finds him not guilty later on, the Ministry of Justice foots the bill.

If, on the other hand, the case is one that the Police Judiciaire has investigated on its own initiative and if, in the end, there is no crime and hence no culprit, any costs become the responsibility of the Préfecture, which is to say the Ministry of the Interior.

And yet, for the police officers, this makes a huge difference. The courts, which always assume that the criminal will pay, are not too fussy, and will generally pay for a taxi. The Préfecture, on the contrary, goes through the expenses forms with a fine-tooth comb and requires accounts for the slightest comings and goings that cost the public purse money.

In this instance, was Maigret not working to ensure that there was neither a crime nor a culprit?

That would therefore mean no expenses, or expenses that were as modest as possible, and he knew that if nothing came of it he would have to justify the use of his men.

'Let's go!'

There was no snow, contrary to the forecast on the radio, but a cold, yellowish fog. The two men, in the light and heat of the Brasserie Dauphine, didn't have beers, which seemed inappropriate to the season, but aperitifs. Leaning on the bar, they didn't talk about Marton, they chatted a little with the owner, after which, with the collars of their overcoats turned up, they returned to the office.

Maigret had decided to leave the door to the inspectors' office half open and to put Lapointe, who was quite good at shorthand, behind the door. It was a precaution, just in case.

At 6.50 he was sitting at his desk, waiting for old Joseph to knock on the door. At 6.55 he was still waiting, and Lapointe, clutching a well-sharpened pencil, was also waiting behind the door.

Maigret was beginning to get impatient when, at seven o'clock, he heard some footsteps at last, familiar little taps, and saw the white porcelain handle turning.

It was Joseph. Having been warned in advance, he merely whispered:

'It's the gentleman you're waiting for.'

'Show him in.'

'Sorry for being a bit late . . .' Marton said. 'There was no point taking the Métro at this time of day . . . There were two full buses, and I came on foot, thinking that that would be quicker . . .'

He was slightly out of breath and seemed to be hot from running.

'If you would like to take off your coat . . .'

'That might be a good idea. I think I'm starting to get a cold . . .'

It took some time for him to sort himself out. He didn't know where to put his overcoat. At first he put it on a chair, then noticed that that was the one he was supposed to sit on if he was to face the inspector, so he carried it to the other end of the room.

At last they were sitting face to face, Maigret smoking his pipe and studying his visitor more intensely than he had the previous day. He was almost disappointed. For twenty-four hours his thoughts had revolved around Marton, who had in the end been transformed into an extraordinary character, and the man in front of him was completely ordinary, like hundreds of others one might bump into on the Métro or in the street.

He was a little put out with him for being so banal, for behaving in such a natural manner.

'I'm sorry again for leaving your office without warning you. Discipline is strict at the store. I had been given permission to leave for an hour to go to my dentist, who lives on Rue Saint-Roch, a stone's throw from the Louvre. Once I was here I immediately realized that time was passing, and that I had to be at my post for a delivery of merchandise at eleven o'clock. I planned to give a message to your office boy, the old man who let me in, but he wasn't in the corridor. I should have phoned you, but we are forbidden to make private calls, and most of the telephones go through the switchboard.'

'How did you manage to do that this afternoon?'

'I took advantage of the fact that there was no one in the floor manager's office, where there is a direct line. You will have noticed that I was in a hurry to say what I had to say and hung up abruptly . . .'

Nothing extraordinary about any of that.

'At midday, when you went for lunch . . .' Maigret objected.

'First of all, I told myself that you would be busy having lunch as well. Then it seemed to me that you wouldn't take my case very seriously . . .'

'And is it serious?'

'Certainly. It was you who sent someone to prowl around my department, wasn't it?'

Maigret didn't reply. The other man went on:

'You don't want to say so, but I'm sure it was an inspector.'

He must have prepared this conversation just as he had prepared the first one. But there were moments of hesitation, like empty spaces. He hesitated for a long time before asking:

'Did my wife come to see you?'

'What makes you think that?'

'I don't know. I've known her for a long time. I'm sure

she suspects something. Women have antennae. And with her character, if she senses the slightest danger, she will attack. Do you understand what I mean?'

A silence, during which he observed Maigret reproachfully, as if he was angry with him for not being open.

'Did she come?'

Maigret hesitated in turn, realizing that he was assuming a great deal of responsibility. If Marton was, to any degree, mentally ill, the answer might have a huge influence on his future behaviour.

Just now, alone in his office, Maigret had nearly phoned his friend Pardon to request his presence at the interview. But had the doctor not already told him that he knew practically nothing about psychiatry?

Xavier Marton was there, on his chair, a metre and a half away from the inspector, talking and behaving like any visitor. Perhaps he was a normal man, who felt that his life was in danger and had come in good faith to inform the police.

Perhaps, on the other hand, he was a man obsessed and suffering from persecution mania, who needed reassurance. Perhaps he was a madman.

And perhaps, finally, he was a man tormented by diabolical ideas, a lunatic too, in a sense, but a lucid, intelligent lunatic, having constructed a minutely detailed plan that he would put into action whatever the cost.

His face was ordinary. He had a nose, eyes, a mouth, ears like everyone. The blood had gone to his head, because of the contrast between the cold outside and the warmth of the office, and perhaps that was what made his eyes glisten, or perhaps it was the head cold that he had spoken of.

Was he really starting to have a head cold, or had he only mentioned it because he knew his eyes would be glistening?

Maigret was uneasy. He was beginning to suspect that the man had come only to ask him the question about his wife.

Had he spied on her in turn? Did he know that she had come to Quai des Orfèvres and did he hope to learn what she had said?

'She came,' Maigret said at last.

'What did she tell you?'

'Usually we're the ones who ask the questions here, we don't answer them.'

'Forgive me.'

'Your wife is very elegant, Monsieur Marton.'

Marton drew his lips back mechanically in something resembling a smile, with a hint of irony or bitterness.

'I know. She has always dreamed of being elegant. She decided to be elegant.'

He had stressed the word *decided* as if underlining it in a letter, and Maigret remembered that his interlocutor had stressed a word before.

Had he not read, in his psychiatric textbook, that stressing words was often a sign of . . .

But he refused to put the discussion on that level.

'Yesterday morning you came to tell me that you feared for your life. You spoke of the attitude that your wife had had for some time, a toxic substance that you found in a cupboard. You also told me that several times, after meals, you felt indisposed. While we're on that subject, I was called in to see the commissioner, and our conversation did not resume, because you had left. I assume you have other details to pass on to me?'

Marton had the slightly sad smile of a man who is being unfairly given a rough ride.

'There is a way of asking questions that makes them difficult to answer,' he remarked.

Maigret almost lost his temper, because he felt as if he was being taught a lesson and was aware that he deserved it.

'But damn it all, you aren't going to tell me that you came here with no particular purpose in mind? Are you bringing a complaint against your wife?'

Marton shook his head.

'You're not accusing her?'

'Of what?' he asked.

'If what you have told me is true, you could accuse her of attempted murder.'

'Do you really think that would lead to a result? What proof do I have? You yourself don't believe me. I gave you a sample of zinc phosphide, but I could just as easily have put it in the broom cupboard myself. The fact that I went of my own accord to see a neurologist will lead to the conclusion that I am not of entirely sound mind, or indeed, and this would be equally plausible, that I am trying to give that impression.'

It was the first time that Maigret had faced a client like this and he couldn't help looking at him with astonishment.

Each answer, each new attitude disconcerted him. He tried in vain to find a flaw, a weak point, and invariably he was the one who was put in his place.

'I'm sure my wife will have talked to you about my nervous exhaustion. She will also have told you that sometimes in the evening, when I am tinkering, I stamp my feet and burst into tears because I can't turn my ideas into reality . . .'

'Did you talk to Doctor Steiner about that?'

'I told him everything. For an hour he asked me questions that would never have occurred to you.'

'So?'

He looked Maigret straight in the eyes.

'So, I'm not mad.'

'But you're still convinced that your wife is trying to kill you?'

'Yes.'

'But you don't want us to open an investigation?'

'There would be no point.'

'And you don't want us to protect you?'

'How would you do that?'

'So, once more, why are you here?'

'So that you know. So that if anything bad happens to me people don't assume a natural death, as they would if I hadn't alerted you. I've read a lot about poisonings. According to your own experts, out of every ten criminal poisonings, nine go undetected and therefore unpunished.'

'Where did you read that?'

'In a journal of forensics.'

'Are you a subscriber?'

'No. I read it in a public library. Now I can tell you one last thing: I don't plan to let it happen.'

Maigret gave a start, feeling that at last they were getting to the heart of the matter.

'What do you mean exactly?'

'First of all, that I'm taking precautions, as I told you yesterday. And then that precisely because of the statistic that I have just quoted I wouldn't trust the legal system and, if I have time, I will take justice into my own hands.'

'Do I take it you mean that you will kill your wife *in advance*?'

'Before dying, of course, but not before she has succeeded in poisoning me. Few poisons cause a violent death, and more or less all of them are very difficult to get hold of. So a certain amount of time will pass between the moment when I know she has succeeded and the moment when I will be incapable of action. I have a loaded revolver at home. It is also properly registered, you can check at city hall. My wife knows, because I've had it for years. Except that for some time it's been hidden in a place where she won't find it. She has looked for it. She's still looking . . .'

There were moments when Maigret wondered if he wouldn't be better off driving his man to the police special infirmary straight away.

'Let's imagine that tonight, half an hour after your dinner, you felt stomach pains?'

'Don't worry, Monsieur Maigret. I am capable of telling the difference between poisoning and simple indigestion. And besides, I have always had a very strong stomach.'

'But if you thought you had been poisoned, you would act?'

'If I *feel* poisoned, I won't hesitate.'

'You'll shoot?'

'Yes.'

The telephone rang, and it seemed to Maigret that it made an unfamiliar din in the room, in which a heavy, tense, almost unhealthy atmosphere now reigned.

'It's Lucas, chief . . .'

'Yes . . .'

'I couldn't put you in the picture before, because I didn't want to leave her alone on the embankment . . .'

'Who?'

'The wife . . . Let me explain . . . I had to wait for an inspector to pass by where I was standing so that he could take over and I could come and phone you . . . It was Torrence who took my place . . .'

'Hurry up. Don't talk too loudly, because you're making the receiver vibrate . . .'

Had Marton worked out that this was indirectly about him?

'Understood, chief . . . Well . . . ! Janvier pointed out your man as soon as he was leaving the shop . . . I started following him, alone, while Janvier was waiting for a bus . . .'

'And then?'

'While we were walking in the crowd, which is dense at that time of day, I didn't notice anything. But crossing the courtyard of the Louvre, and then reaching the riverside, I realized that I wasn't the only one following him . . .'

'Go on.'

'There was a woman on his heels . . . I don't think she noticed me, but I'm not sure . . . She followed him to Quai des Orfèvres and she's still there, about a hundred metres from the entrance . . .'

'Describe her . . .'

'It's not worth it. When Torrence passed by me and I let him take over, I came up here and asked Janvier to go and look down, given that he's been dealing with the case . . . He's just come back up and he's right here . . . Do you want me to pass him to you?'

'Yes.'

'Hello, chief . . . ! It's the sister-in-law, Jenny . . .'

'You're sure?'

'Certain.'

'She didn't recognize you?'

'No. I've been careful.'

'Thank you.'

'No instructions?'

'Let Torrence keep on watching her.'

'And what about the man? Is Lucas to go on following him when he comes out?'

'Yes.'

He hung up and found Marton's quizzical eyes fixed on him.

'Is it my wife?' the train-set lover asked.

'What do you mean?'

'Nothing. I should know that you wouldn't tell me the truth anyway.'

'Did you hear?'

'No, except it isn't hard to work out. If it is my wife . . .'

'Well?'

'Nothing. I was wrong to come and see you yesterday, and all the more so today. Since you don't believe me . . .'

'All I want is to believe you. Here you are: because you're sure of yourself, I'm going to make you a proposition. Doctor Steiner, bound by patient confidentiality, won't tell me anything.'

'Do you want me to be examined by another doctor?'

'By the specialist at the police infirmary. He is a man of integrity, a world-famous professor.'

'When? Right now?'

Was Maigret mistaken? Was his interlocutor experiencing a moment of panic?

'No. He mustn't be disturbed at this time of day. He will be on duty tomorrow morning.'

Marton calmly replied:

'As long as it isn't too early, I'll have time to tell the shop.'

'So you agree?'

'Why wouldn't I?'

'Do you also agree to sign a piece of paper testifying that you are making this visit entirely of your own accord?'

'If you wish.'

'You are a curious man, Monsieur Marton.'

'Do you think so?'

'You are here of your own accord as well, I haven't forgotten that. So you aren't obliged to answer my questions. However, I have a few that I would like to ask you.'

'Will you believe my answers?'

'I will try to, and I can assure you that I'm not prejudiced against you.'

That declaration provoked only an embittered smile.

'Do you love your wife?'

'Now?'

'Now, of course.'

'Then no.'

'Does she love you?'

'She hates me.'

'That's not the image I had of you as a couple when you left her yesterday morning.'

'We didn't have time to get to the bottom of things, and in any case you didn't want to.'

'As you wish. Shall I go on?'

'Please do.'

'Did you love her?'

'I thought I did.'

'Tell me what you mean by that.'

'Until that point I had lived alone, without allowing myself the slightest distraction. I worked a lot, you know. Coming from as close to the bottom as I did, it took an enormous effort to become what I became.'

'You had never had any relationships with women when you met your wife?'

'Rarely. The kind of affairs that I'm sure you can guess. I felt more shame than pleasure. Then, when I met Gisèle, I turned her into the ideal woman and it was that ideal woman that I loved. The word "couple" was a prestigious one for me. I dreamed of it. We were going to be a couple. I was going to become one half of a couple. I would no longer be alone in my home, in life. And one day, we would have children . . .'

'You don't have any?'

'Gisèle doesn't want to.'

'Did she warn you?'

'No. If she had warned me, I would have married her anyway, and settled for being a couple . . .'

'Did she love you?'

'I thought so.'

'And then one day you noticed that you were mistaken?'

'Yes.'

'When?'

He didn't reply straight away. All of a sudden he found himself facing a serious dilemma and as he was thinking. Maigret didn't press him.

'I assume,' Marton murmured at last, 'that you've carried out investigations? If you had sent someone to spy on me at the shop, you must also have sent one of your men to Avenue de Châtillon.'

'Correct.'

'In that case I should speak frankly. In answer to the question you asked me: two years ago.'

'In other words, at more or less the same time that your sister-in-law came to live in your household you worked out that your wife didn't love you and that she had never loved you?'

'Yes.'

'Can you explain why?'

'It's easy. Before I knew my sister-in-law, who lived in

America with her husband, I wasn't always happy at home, but I told myself I was as happy as you can be. Do you understand? In other words, I considered my feelings of disillusion to be inevitable, imagining that all men were in the same situation as me. In short, Gisèle was a woman, and I had come to believe that her shortcomings were those inherent in all women.'

He was still choosing his words carefully, pronouncing some of them more emphatically than others.

'Like everyone else, I suppose, I had dreamed of a certain form of love, of union, fusion, call it what you will, and after several years or several months I reached the conclusion that it doesn't exist.'

'So, you'd decided that love doesn't exist.'

'That sort of love, in any case.'

'What do you not like about your wife?'

'You seem to want me to be ungentlemanly, but if I don't reply honestly you will draw false conclusions. I know today, for example, that when Gisèle left Rouen and her family it was only out of ambition. Not out of love of the man she followed back then, and who dropped her after a few months, as she wanted to have me believe. That man was the first rung on the ladder, he represented Paris. Even if he hadn't left her, she wouldn't have stayed with him for long.'

It was strange to hear him talking like this, without fire, without passion, as if he were studying an impersonal case, trying to be clear and precise.

'Except, she imagined that it would all happen more quickly. She was young, pretty, desirable. She didn't expect she'd be running from outer office to outer office and copying down job adverts in the newspaper windows before ending up in the lingerie department of a big store.'

'Aren't you ambitious too?'

'There's no comparison. Let me finish telling you about her. She went out in the evening with colleagues, particularly with the heads of department, but either they were married or they didn't propose to her. It was at that moment, just as she felt herself growing old, that I appeared on the scene. Three or four years earlier she would have made fun of me. Experience had taught her that I was an acceptable last resort and she did what she had to do.'

'Which is to say?'

'She let me believe that she loved me. For years I thought only of the couple that we formed together, what we called our nest, what I also called our future. I found her cold, but I consoled myself by thinking that women who aren't cold are playing a part. I found her self-seeking, even greedy, and I also convinced myself that all women are.'

'Were you unhappy?'

'I had my work. She laughed at me, calling me a lunatic. She was ashamed, I know now, to be married to a man who dealt with children's toys and train sets. She had found something better.'

Maigret could see what was coming.

'What do you mean?'

'She made the acquaintance of a man who worked at the shop for a while, one Maurice Schwob. I don't know if she loves him. It's possible. He at least enabled her to take a step further, and a big step at that. He married a former actress who was a kept woman for a long time and who has lots of money . . .'

'Is that why your wife didn't ask for a divorce with a view to marrying Schwob?'

'I imagine so. However, they did set up a shop together with the old woman's money.'

'Do you think they're lovers?'

'I know they are.'

'Have you followed them?'

'I'm as curious as anyone.'

'But you haven't asked for a divorce?'

He didn't reply. They seemed to have reached an impasse.

'Did that situation exist even before your sister-in-law came on the scene?'

'Probably, but my eyes hadn't been opened yet.'

'You said just now that since your sister-in-law has been living with you on Avenue de Châtillon you've understood. Understood what?'

'That there are other kinds of women, women like the ones I've always dreamed of.'

'Do you love her?'

'Yes.'

'Is she your mistress?'

'No.'

'And yet you sometimes meet her without your wife's knowledge?'

'You know that too?'

'I know of the little restaurant called Le Trou Normand.'

'It's true. Jenny often comes and joins me there at lunch-time. My wife almost always goes to the most luxurious places with Schwob. She's no longer part of our world, do you understand?'

That last word returned frequently, as if Marton was worried that Maigret was incapable of following him.

'Does your sister-in-law love you too?'

'I think she's starting to.'

'Just starting to?'

'She really loved her husband. They were a true couple. They lived in New Jersey, not far from New York, in a pretty house in the country. Edgard was killed in an accident, and Jenny tried to kill herself. She turned on the gas one evening and was saved just in time. So, not knowing what to do, she came back to Europe, and we took her in. She was still in mourning. She can't get used to wearing anything but mourning. Gisèle makes fun of her, advises her to go out and enjoy herself, to get out of her rut. On the other hand I'm very gently trying to give her back her taste for life . . .'

'Have you managed to do that?'

He blushed like a teenager.

'I think so. Now you understand why she isn't my mistress? I love and respect her. I wouldn't, for some kind of selfish satisfaction, want to . . .'

Was Lapointe recording all this? If this interrogation had been conducted regularly, Maigret would have looked utterly ridiculous.

'Does Jenny know that her sister wants you dead?'

'I haven't talked to her about it.'

'Does she know that you're unhappy?'

'She lives with us. I should point out that my wife and I never argue. To all appearances, we lead the life of an ordinary married couple. Gisèle is too intelligent to start rows. And there's ten million at stake, which would allow her to become an equal partner in the business on Rue Saint-Honoré, with that man Schwob, who has changed his name to Harris.'

'What ten million is that?'

'The money from the insurance.'

'When did you take out insurance? Before or after the arrival of your sister-in-law?'

'Before. About four years ago now. Gisèle was already working with Schwob. An insurance salesman paid us a visit as if by chance, but I understood later that it was my wife who had asked him to come. You know how it goes. "You don't know who will live or who will die," he said. "It's a comfort for the one who goes to know that the one who stays . . ."'

He laughed, for the first time, an unpleasant little laugh.

'I didn't yet know at the time. In short, we ended up signing a policy for ten million.'

'You say *we*?'

'Yes, because it's a joint policy, as they say.'

'In other words if your wife dies, you too will get hold of ten million?'

'Of course.'

'So that you gain as much from her death as she does from yours?'

'I can't hide it.'

'And you hate each other?'

'She hates me, yes.'

'And you?'

'I don't hate her. I just take my precautions.'

'But you love your sister-in-law.'

'I won't hide that either.'

'And your wife is Schwob-Harris' mistress.'

'That's a fact.'

'Have you anything else to tell me?'

'I don't think so. I've answered your questions. I think I've even gone beyond some of them. I'm ready, tomorrow morning, to take the test that you talked to me about. At what time do I have to be here?'

'Between ten and midday. Which time suits you better?'

'Will it take long?'

'About as long as your session at Doctor Steiner's.'

'An hour, then. Let's say eleven, if you like. That way I won't need to go back to the shop.'

He was rising hesitantly to his feet, perhaps waiting for new questions. As he put on his overcoat, Maigret murmured:

'Your sister-in-law is waiting for you by the river.'

He stopped for a moment with his arm in the air, the sleeve of his coat half on.

'Ah!'

'Does that surprise you? So she didn't know you were coming here?'

There was a second's hesitation, but it didn't escape Maigret.

'Obviously not.'

This time he was lying, it was obvious. He was suddenly in a great hurry to leave. He was no longer as sure of himself as he had been a moment before.

'See you tomorrow . . .' he stammered.

And since he had automatically begun to hold out his hand, he had to take it to its conclusion. Maigret shook the hand that was extended to him, watched Marton heading for the stairs, closed the door and stood behind it for a while, inhaling deeply.

'Ouf . . . !' he sighed while Lapointe, with an aching wrist, appeared in the doorway opposite.

He couldn't remember a more unsettling interrogation.

6. An Evening at the Cinema

'Lucas?' Maigret asked, nodding towards the connecting door between the two offices.

Not only did Lapointe understand the meaning of the question, he understood that at that moment the chief had no desire to form long sentences.

'He went to take Torrence's place on the embankment. Since Torrence wasn't in the picture . . .'

Maigret abruptly changed the subject, and once again Lapointe followed him without difficulty.

'What do you think?

Apart from Janvier, whom he had always addressed as a familiar, Maigret used the informal *tu* with only a very few people, and then only in the heat of action, or when he was very worried. Lapointe was always pleased when it happened, because it was a little as if the two men were suddenly exchanging confidences.

'I don't know, chief, I was listening but couldn't see him, and the two things are very different.'

That was exactly why Maigret was asking him his advice. They had heard the same words. But the young man, behind the door, had not been distracted by a face, eyes, hands as Maigret had been. He felt a little as if he was in the situation one of the usherettes in the theatre, who hears the play from the corridors, and for whom the soliloquies have a different resonance.

'He sounded sincere to me.'

'Not slightly mad?'

'It must be difficult to explain yourself, with someone like you sitting right in front of you . . .'

Lapointe had hesitated before saying that for fear of being misunderstood, even though in his mind it was a compliment.

'You will have a clearer understanding of what I mean when you read through your replies. It's only at the end . . .'

'What do you mean, at the end?'

'. . . that he was probably lying. At least from my point of view. The sister-in-law must have known he was coming here. He knew she knew. What he didn't know was that she had followed him and was waiting for him on the embankment. I think that made him angry. Do you want me to type the text out straight away?'

Maigret shook his head and added:

'I hope you won't need to type it out.'

Maigret was starting to lose patience and wondered why Lucas wasn't coming back up. There was no reason to follow the couple to Avenue de Châtillon. Maigret couldn't wait to know how the encounter had gone, and Lapointe shared his curiosity.

'I wonder,' Lapointe murmured, 'why he claimed that his sister-in-law knew nothing about it.'

'There may be a reason.'

'What?'

'His desire not to compromise her, to ensure that she isn't accused of complicity one day.'

'But she could only be complicit if . . .'

Lapointe broke off and looked at his boss with surprise. Maigret's words assumed that something was going to happen, something that would make Xavier Marton look bad. There was no time to talk about it any further, because they heard the sound of quick, short footsteps that could only have belonged to Lucas. He passed through the inspectors' office and stood framed in the half-open door.

'Can I come in, chief?'

He was still wearing his overcoat, a black overcoat in a woollen fabric on which some tiny white dots were still visible.

'Is it snowing?'

'It's starting to. Fine snow, but icy.'

'Tell us.'

'The girl down on the embankment can't have been any warmer than me, particularly since she's wearing light shoes, and I heard her heels striking the cobbles. At first she stood motionless by the stone parapet, avoiding the streetlights. From the way she was standing I could tell, even though I could only see her silhouette, that she was looking at the windows where the lights were on. There aren't many of those left in the building. I saw them going out one by one myself. From time to time voices could be heard from the entrance. I'd never realized that our voices carry so far when we leave here. Inspectors were coming out in groups of two or three, wishing each other good evening, heading off home . . .

'She approached very gradually, as if fascinated by the lights of your office, and she was becoming more and more nervous. I'm sure that several times she was on the point of crossing the road and coming in . . .'

'She must have imagined that I'd arrested him?'

'I don't know. Finally he came out on his own, passing in front of the officer on guard duty. All of a sudden he cast his eyes around, as if looking for somebody . . .'

'He was looking for her. I'd just told him she was there.'

'Now I understand. It was hard for him to see her where she was standing. At first he looked for her in the direction of Pont-Neuf, but she was standing in the opposite direction. He turned on his heels. I thought she was going to take advantage of the moment when his back was turned to leave, or go down to the unloading quay, but he spotted her before she moved. I couldn't hear what they were saying. From their postures, I thought I could tell that he was rebuking her for something. He wasn't gesticulating, but his posture was that of an angry man.

'She was the one who slipped her hand under his arm, pointing to the sentry, and led him towards Pont Saint-Michel . . .'

'Just one moment,' Maigret broke in. 'How exactly did she slip her hand under his arm?'

Lucas seemed not to understand the point of the question, but Lapointe, who was in love, did.

'Quite naturally, like the women you see in the street with their lover or their husband. He must have told her off again, but less energetically. Then I assume he noticed that she was cold and put his arm around her waist. They pressed their bodies a little more closely together and began to walk at the same pace, in the same rhythm . . .'

Lapointe and Maigret looked at each other, thinking the same thing.

'When they reached Pont Saint-Michel they paused for a moment and then, following the line of cars, and still with their arms around each other's waist, they went into the bar on the corner. There were lots of people at the counter. It was aperitif time. I saw them through the misted windows. I didn't go in. They were both standing by the till. The waiter made a hot rum and set it down on the bar in front of the young woman, who seemed to protest. Marton insisted. In the end she drank the rum, blowing on it, while he settled for a coffee.'

'Out of interest,' Maigret asked Lapointe, 'what did he drink at lunchtime, at the restaurant?'

'Mineral water.'

That was strange. Had he been asked the question, Maigret would in fact have wagered that the train-set lover drank neither wine nor spirits.

'When they came out,' Lucas said, finishing his report, 'they made for the bus stop and waited. I saw them board a bus heading towards Porte d'Orléans and I thought it would be better for me to come and tell you. Did I do the right thing?'

Maigret nodded. The snow had disappeared from Lucas' overcoat; during the conversation he had warmed his hands at the radiator.

Then Maigret was addressing him by the informal *tu* as well.

'Do you have anything planned for this evening?'

'Nothing special.'

'Me neither,' Lapointe said hastily.

'I don't know which one of you I'm going to ask to spend the night outside. It won't be much fun in this weather . . .'

'Me . . . !' said the young inspector, raising his hand like a schoolboy.

And Lucas said:

'Why don't we share the shift? You can phone my wife to tell her I won't be home for dinner. I'm going to have a sandwich in a bar, opposite the Montrouge church. Later Lapointe can come and relieve me . . .'

'I'll be there at about ten o'clock,' Lapointe decided.

'Later if you like. Why not cut the night in two and call it midnight?'

'No, I'll be there a bit earlier. If I'm not going to bed, I like to have something to do.'

'What are your instructions, chief?'

'None. And tomorrow, if they ask me to give an account myself, I'll be hard pushed to explain the reasons for this watch. They both came here, the husband and the wife. They were both keen to inform me about their little disputes. Logically, nothing should happen. But that's exactly because . . .'

He didn't finish his thought, which was no clearer for having been expressed in words.

'Perhaps I was wrong to tell him his wife had come here. I hesitated. Then I said to myself . . .'

He shrugged with exasperation and opened the cupboard where he kept his overcoat and hat, grumbling:

'Well! We'll see . . . Goodnight anyway, boys . . .'

'Goodnight, chief.'

And Lucas added:

'I'll be down there in an hour.'

Outside, the cold had become more acute, and the snowflakes, tiny and hard, barely visible in the halo of the streetlights, prickled the skin as if trying to cling there, settled on the eyelashes, the eyebrows, the lips.

Maigret couldn't face waiting for a bus so he took a taxi and huddled on the back seat, well wrapped up in his heavy coat.

All his previous investigations seemed almost childishly simple in comparison with this one, and he was irritated about it. He had never felt less confident about himself, so much so that he had phoned Pardon, gone to see the chief and the public prosecutor and, just now, sought Lapointe's approval.

He felt he was floundering. Then, as the taxi drove around Place de la République, he had a thought which put his mind somewhat at rest.

If this investigation wasn't like the others and he didn't know how to approach it, wasn't it because this time it wasn't a crime that had been committed and only had to be reconstructed, but a crime that could be committed at any moment?

Just as it was quite possible that it wouldn't be committed at all! How many potential crimes, crimes in waiting, some of them worked out down to the tiniest detail in the criminal's mind, are never actually perpetrated? How many people plan to get rid of someone, imagine all the possible ways by which they might achieve their ends, before pulling back at the last minute?

Cases that he had dealt with came back into his mind. Some of them would never have reached their conclusion without a favourable opportunity, sometimes without a fortuitous event. In certain cases, if, at a given moment, the victim hadn't uttered a particular phrase, adopted a particular attitude, nothing would have happened.

What he had to do this time was not to reconstruct the actions and gestures of a human being, but to predict his behaviour, which was difficult in a different way.

None of the textbooks on psychology, psychoanalysis and psychiatry were of any use to him.

He had known other couples one half of which had, for some reason, wished for the death of the other.

Those precedents were of no use to him either. Precedents are only useful with professionals, or with certain kinds of maniac. And even then only with maniacs who have killed several times before and who go on to do it again.

He didn't notice that the taxi had stopped by the kerb. The driver said:

'We're here, chief.'

The door to the flat opened as usual, and Maigret found the light, the familiar smells, the furniture and the objects that had been in place for so many years.

He also found the face of Madame Maigret, which, as always, and particularly when she knew he was worried, contained a mute question.

'Why don't we go to the cinema?' he suggested.

'It's snowing!'

'Are you scared of getting cold?'

'No. I'd love to go to the cinema.'

She suspected that he didn't want to sit in his armchair ruminating on a question going round in his head over and over again as he had done the day before. An hour later they were walking towards Place de la République and Boulevard Bonne-Nouvelle, and Madame Maigret had linked arms with her husband.

Xavier Marton's sister-in-law, Jenny, had done the same thing when he had surprised her by the river. Maigret wondered how much time had passed after their first meeting before his wife had done the same.

About a hundred metres away from the cinema, where he didn't even know what film they were showing, he asked her.

'I know,' she said smiling. 'I remember exactly. We had known each other for three months. The previous week you had kissed me on the landing, and after that you kissed me every evening in the same place. One Tuesday you took me to the Opéra Comique, where they were performing *Carmen*, and I was wearing a blue taffeta dress. I could tell you what perfume I had put on. On the way to the taxi you didn't put your arm around me, you just held out your hand to help me into the car.

'After the theatre you asked me if I was hungry. We went to the Grands Boulevards, where the Taverne Pousset used to be.

'I pretended to stumble because of my high heels and rested my hand on your arm. I was so impressed by my audacity that I was trembling, and you had the good idea of pretending you hadn't noticed a thing.

'As we left the restaurant I did the same thing again, and since then I've done it all the time.'

In other words Jenny too had the same habit. It meant that she and her brother-in-law often walked along the street together.

Didn't that suggest that they weren't hiding, and Gisèle Marton knew all about it, contrary to what her husband said?

He leaned towards the ticket kiosk, then made for the entrance with two pink tickets in his hand.

It was a thriller, with gunshots and fights, and a hard-boiled hero jumping out of a window only to land in a convertible and then, in the middle of the city, knocking out the driver, taking the steering wheel and driving at a crazy speed, escaping the police cars with their wailing sirens.

He smiled in spite of himself. Basically he was having fun. He forgot the Martons and the sister-in-law, Harris whose name was Schwob and the somewhat complicated relationships of the two couples.

At the interval he bought some sweets for his wife, a tradition that went back almost as long as her taking him by the arm. Another tradition was that while she ate her sweets he smoked half a pipe in the foyer, looking vaguely at the posters of the coming attractions.

The snow was still falling when they came out, and the flakes were thicker now, trembling on the ground for a moment before dissolving.

People walked with their heads bowed so that the flakes didn't get in their eyes. Tomorrow, in all probability, the snow would whiten the roofs and the parked cars.

'Taxi!'

He was worried that his wife might catch a chill. He thought that she had already lost weight, and even though he knew that this was on the instructions of Pardon it still worried him. He was concerned that she would become frailer and perhaps lose her optimism and her good humour.

As the car stopped opposite their flat on Boulevard Richard-Lenoir, he murmured:

'Would it bother you a lot if I came back in an hour?'

In any other case he wouldn't have asked her the question. He would just have announced what he had to do. This evening it was an initiative that wasn't necessary, for which there was in fact no reason, and he felt the need to apologize for it.

'Shall I wait up for you?'

'No. Go to bed. I may be late.'

He saw her crossing the pavement, looking in her bag for the key to the flat.

'The church of Saint-Pierre de Montrouge,' he said to the driver.

The streets were almost empty, the cobbles slippery, with huge marks left by cars that had zigzagged.

'Not too fast . . .'

He thought:

'What if something really does happen . . .'

Why did he feel it would happen very soon? Xavier

Marton had come to see him the previous day. Not a week sooner, while the situation was the same, but only the previous day. Did that not suggest that the drama was reaching its conclusion?

Gisèle had come to police headquarters the previous day as well.

And her husband had returned today.

He tried to remember what they had said about this in the psychiatry book that he had skimmed through. Perhaps, after all, he had been wrong not to take a greater interest? There had been several pages on the evolution of acute crises, but he had skipped those.

And yet, there was something that could hasten the drama, if indeed there was a drama. Xavier Marton had agreed to take a test, the next day, at eleven o'clock in the morning, at the special police infirmary.

Would he tell his sister-in-law about it? His wife? Would his wife pass on the news to her lover on Rue Saint-Honoré?

Once he had taken the test, whatever the results, it seemed that it would be too late for any new developments.

The taxi stopped in front of the church. Maigret paid his fare. Opposite, a bar was still open, with only two or three customers inside. Maigret pushed the door open, ordered a hot rum, not so much to warm himself up as because someone had mentioned hot rum a short time before. As he was heading for the telephone cabin, the waiter called to him:

'Do you want a token?'

'I just want to take a look at the directory.'

For no precise reason, in fact. Thinking of Monsieur Harris, he had wondered whether the Martons had a telephone and he was going to check.

They didn't. Lots of Mortons, Martins, but not a single Marton.

'How much do I owe you?'

He stepped outside into Avenue de Châtillon, which was deserted, and where no more than two or three windows were lit. He could see neither Lucas nor Lapointe, and he was starting to get worried when, towards the middle of the avenue, just past Rue Antoine-Chantin, he heard a nearby voice saying:

'Here, chief . . .'

It was young Lapointe, huddled in a corner with a scarf pulled up to the middle of his face, his hands plunged deep in his coat pockets.

'I recognized your footsteps as soon as you turned the corner of the avenue.'

'Is that it?' Maigret asked, nodding towards a yellow brick building with all its windows in darkness.

'Yes. You see that dark hole to the right of the door?'

It was a kind of blind alley, a passage of the sort one still sees often in Paris, even in the heart of the city. It was in just such a passage on Boulevard Saint-Martin that a murdered man had once been found, at five o'clock in the afternoon, a few metres from the crowd passing along the pavement.

'Does it lead to the courtyard?'

'Yes. They can go in and out without calling the concierge.'

'Did you go and see?'

'I go there every ten minutes. If you go, be careful. There's a huge ginger cat that comes over silently and rubs itself against your legs. The first time it miaowed, and I was worried that it was going to sound the alarm.'

'Have they gone to bed?'

'They hadn't just now.'

'What are they doing?'

'I don't know. There must be someone on the first floor, but you can't see anything because of the blinds. I waited in vain to see a silhouette, like a shadow puppet; it looks as if the person or people who are in the room aren't moving, or else they're staying on the far side. The ground floor is lit as well. You only realize that after a while, because the mechanical shutters only let out thin chinks of light.'

Maigret crossed the street, and Lapointe followed him. They were both careful not to make any noise. The passageway, which was arched for about three or four metres, was as cold and damp as a cellar. They found the courtyard in total darkness and, while they stood motionless, a cat did in fact come and rub itself not against Maigret, but Lapointe, whom it seemed already to have adopted.

'They've gone to bed,' Lapointe whispered. 'The window with the light on was just in front of you.'

On tiptoes, he approached the shutters on the ground floor, bent down and came back towards Maigret. Just as the two men were preparing to turn around and leave, a light came on, not in the small house, but on the third floor of the block.

They both froze in the shadow, fearing that they might be heard by a tenant, and expected to see a face pressed against the window.

It didn't happen. A shadow passed behind the curtain. They heard the sound of water flushing.

'Somebody having a wee . . .' Lapointe sighed, reassured.

A moment later they were back on the opposite pavement. Curiously, they both felt disappointed. It was Lapointe who murmured:

'They've gone to bed.'

Didn't that mean that nothing was going to happen, that Maigret had been worried about nothing?

'I wonder . . .' Maigret began.

Two policemen on bicycles appeared, cycling straight towards them. They had spotted them in the distance, and from the kerb one of them called in a loud voice.

'What are you up to, you two?'

Maigret stepped forwards. The beam from a torch sought his face. The policeman frowned.

'You're not . . . ? Oh! Forgive me, detective chief inspector . . . I didn't recognize you straight away . . .'

He added, after glancing at the house opposite:

'Do you need a hand?'

'Not for now.'

'Anyway, we pass by every hour.'

The two caped men cycled off, sprinkled with snow, and Maigret joined Lapointe, who hadn't moved.

'What was I saying?'

'You were wondering . . .'

'Oh yes . . . ! I was wondering if the husband and wife still sleep in the same bed.'

'I don't know. From what Janvier told me this afternoon, there's a sofa on the ground floor, which doesn't mean that anyone sleeps there. Logically, if someone does, it should be the sister-in-law, shouldn't it?'

'Goodnight, my friend. Perhaps you can . . .'

He wondered whether to send Lapointe off to bed. What was the point of keeping watch outside a house where nothing was happening?

'If you're hesitating on my account . . .'

Basically, Lapointe would have been annoyed not to be able to do his stakeout to the end.

'Stay if you like. Goodnight. You don't want to come for a drink?'

'I admit that I went for one a few minutes before you arrived. I was able to keep an eye on the street from the bar on the corner.'

By the time Maigret reached Saint-Pierre de Montrouge, the grilles of the Métro were closed, and there was no taxi in sight. He hesitated between making for the Lion de Belfort and taking Avenue du Maine towards Gare Montparnasse. He chose Avenue du Maine because of the station, and in fact soon hailed a taxi that was coming back empty.

'Boulevard Richard-Lenoir.'

He didn't have a key to the flat, but he knew there was one under the doormat. As head of the Crime Squad, he had never thought of telling his wife that the hiding place was illusory at best.

She was asleep, and he was starting to get undressed in the semi-darkness, leaving only the lamp in the corridor lit. A few moments later a voice from the bed asked him:

'Is it late?'

'I don't know. Maybe one thirty . . .'

'You haven't caught a chill?'

'No.'

'You don't want me to make you a herbal tea?'

'Thank you. I had a hot rum just now.'

'And then you went out again?'

They were banal little phrases that he had heard hundreds of times, but they struck him tonight because he wondered if Gisèle had ever uttered them.

Wasn't it in fact, for want of having heard them, that her husband . . .

'You can turn the light on.'

He merely switched on the bedside light on his side of the bed and went and turned out the one in the corridor.

'Have you closed the front door?'

He wouldn't have been surprised, in a few minutes, to hear his wife getting up to go and check.

That was also part of a whole, a whole that Xavier Marton had probably sought, which he hadn't found, which . . .

He slipped between the warm covers, turned the light out and found in the darkness, without having to look very hard, his wife's lips.

He thought he would have trouble getting to sleep but a few moments later he was slumbering. It is true that, if someone had turned on the light abruptly, they would have seen that his face was set in a frown, a concentrated expression, as if he were still in pursuit of a truth that escaped him.

Usually Madame Maigret got up silently at half past six and went to the kitchen without his noticing. He only became aware of the new day when he caught the smell of coffee.

It was the time of day when other windows on Boulevard Richard-Lenoir, and in all the districts of Paris, were lighting up; it was also the time when one heard the footsteps on the pavement of people who got up early.

That day he wasn't pulled from sleep by the familiar smell of coffee, or by the hushed footsteps of his wife. It was the sudden ringing of the telephone that dragged him from the world of the night, and, when he opened his eyes, Madame Maigret, already sitting in the bed, was shaking his shoulder.

'What time is it?' he stammered.

She groped around to find the switch of the bedside light, then the light fell on the alarm-clock, and the hands showed 6.10.

'Hello!' Maigret said in a thick voice. 'Is that you, Lapointe?'

'Inspector Maigret?'

He didn't recognize the voice and frowned.

'Who's speaking?'

'The Police Emergency Service. Inspector Joffre.'

Sometimes, in certain particular cases, he would ask the Police Emergency Service to tell him straight away if something particular occurred. But he had done nothing like that the previous day. He hadn't strung his thoughts together yet. And yet he was hardly surprised.

'What is it, Joffre? Is it Lapointe?'

'What do you mean, Lapointe?'

'Was it Lapointe who asked you to call me?'

'I've heard nothing from Lapointe, just a phone call a moment ago, asking us to pass on a message to you.'

'What message?'

'To go to Avenue de Châtillon straight away . . . Wait! I've jotted down the number . . .'

'I know it. Who was that on the phone?'

'I don't know. They didn't give their name.'

'A man? A woman?'

'A woman. She says you know about it and that you'll know what it means. Apparently she looked for your number in the directory but . . .'

Maigret was ex-directory.

'Is there anything I can do for you?'

Maigret hesitated. He nearly asked Joffre to phone the station in the fourteenth arrondissement so that they could send someone to Avenue de Châtillon. Then, on reflection, he did nothing. Sitting on the edge of the bed, he reached with his toes for his slippers. His wife was already in the kitchen, and he heard the little explosion as she lit the gas to heat the water.

'Nothing, thank you . . .'

What surprised him was that it wasn't Lapointe who called him, when he was the man on the spot.

Which woman would it be? Gisèle Marton? The sister-in-law?

If it was one of the two, she couldn't have left the building, because Lapointe would have noticed and called Maigret in person.

And yet the Martons weren't on the phone.

He called to his wife.

'While I'm getting dressed, could you take a look in the phone book, the section classified by street, and tell me who is listed for 17, Avenue de Châtillon?'

He thought about shaving but decided not to, even though he was repelled by the idea of going out like that, to gain some time.

'Seventeen . . . Here it is . . . Building . . .'

'Fine. That means there's a telephone in the concierge's lodge.'

'I also see one Madame Boussard, a midwife. That's all. You'll have your coffee in two minutes.'

He should have told Joffre to send him one of the cars from Quai des Orfèvres, but now that would take longer than calling a taxi.

Madame Maigret took charge of that. Five minutes later, after burning his mouth on some coffee that was still too hot, he came downstairs.

'Will you phone me?' his wife asked, leaning against the banisters.

It was something she asked very rarely. She must have sensed that he was more worried than usual.

He promised:

'I'll try.'

The taxi arrived. He got in and barely noticed that it had stopped snowing, that there were now traces of white in the street, and on the roofs, but that an icy rain was blackening the cobblestones.

'Avenue de Châtillon.'

He sniffed, because the taxi still smelled of perfume. Perhaps it had just driven home a couple who had spent the night dancing in a cabaret. A little later he bent down to pick up a small pink cotton ball of the kind that grown-ups throw after midnight when drinking champagne.

7. The Spiral Staircase

Maigret had asked to be dropped off on the corner of Avenue de Châtillon and, as in his own part of town, the pavements were empty under the rain; as on Boulevard Richard-Lenoir there were some lights on in the windows, three or four per house. Walking a hundred metres, he saw two coming on and heard the sound of an alarm-clock in a still-darkened ground-floor apartment.

He looked around for Lapointe in his corner, didn't find him and muttered a couple of syllables under his breath, sullen, uneasy, drowsy.

In the corridor of the yellow brick building, at last, he saw a very small woman, with hips as wide as her shoulders, who must have been the concierge, a Métro worker holding an iron box containing his lunch and another woman, an old one, with white hair in curlers, wearing a sky-blue woollen dressing gown and a bright purple shawl.

All three looked at him in silence, and it was only later that he found out what had happened, and knew why Lapointe wasn't on the pavement. For a few moments at the very least, he had felt a great emptiness in his chest, because he had thought that as the result of circumstances that he couldn't guess his inspector might be the victim.

It was, as always, simpler than that. When Gisèle Marton had come to make her call in the concierge's lodge, the concierge had got up to make some coffee but she hadn't yet put out the bins. She had heard a call to the Police Emergency Service, then the message of her tenant, who had come out of the lodge without giving her any information at all.

The concierge, as she did every morning, had gone to open one of the double doors to drag the bins to the pavement. Lapointe was just crossing the street, with the intention of glancing into the courtyard as he had done several times during the night. Because of the phone call that she had just overheard, the concierge had looked at him with suspicion.

'What do you want?'

'I don't suppose anything unusual has happened in the house?'

He showed his badge.

'Are you from the police? There is someone, at the end of the courtyard, who has just called the police. What is the meaning of all this to-do?'

So Lapointe had been led across the courtyard, this time without hiding, and knocked at the door beneath which he saw a chink of light. The three windows on the first floor were also lit.

Maigret didn't need to knock. They had heard his footsteps, and it was Lapointe who opened the door to him from inside, a Lapointe who was pale with exhaustion, and also because of what he had just discovered. He didn't say a word, since the spectacle displayed to his chief spoke for itself.

The sofa in the drawing-room-workshop converted into

a bed, and it was Xavier Marton who was lying on it. The blankets were untidy, the pillow was at an angle, and on the floor, on the beige jute mat, halfway between the bed and the spiral staircase that led to the first floor, the body of the train-set lover lay on his belly, in his pyjamas, face down on the floor.

The red stripes of his pyjamas further emphasized his contorted pose. It looked as if he had collapsed while walking on all fours, and he was completely twisted, his right arm stretched out, his fists clenched, as if in one final effort he had tried to reach for the revolver which also lay on the ground, about twenty centimetres from his fingers.

Maigret didn't ask if he was dead. It was obvious. Three people studied him in silence, because the two women were there, almost as motionless as the corpse, they too in nightwear, with dressing gowns over their nightdresses, bare feet in slippers. Some of Jenny's hair, darker than her sister's, had fallen over her face and hid one of her eyes.

Mechanically, and not thinking about what he was saying, Maigret murmured to Lapointe:

'You haven't touched anything?'

Lapointe shook his head. There were rings under his eyes, and his beard, like the dead man's and Maigret's, had grown during the night.

'Alert the local station. Phone Criminal Records to send photographers and experts at once. And call Doctor Paul . . .'

'And the prosecutor's office?'

'There will be time for that later.'

In that part of the Palais de Justice, life didn't begin as early as it did at Quai des Orfèvres, and Maigret didn't want to have those gentlemen under his feet too soon.

He looked at the two women out of the corner of his eye. It hadn't occurred to either of them to sit down. Leaning against the wall, near the table with the train set, the sister-in-law, with a rolled-up handkerchief in her hand, dabbed her red eyes from time to time and sniffed as if she had a head cold. She had big, dark, gentle, fearful eyes, like those of forest animals, roe deer, for example, and she gave off a warm smell of bed.

Colder, or more composed, Gisèle Marton looked at Maigret, and she clenched her hands involuntarily from time to time.

Lapointe had gone outside and walked across the courtyard. He must have been telephoning from the concierge's lodge. The two women probably expected Maigret to question them. Perhaps he had thought for a moment about doing so but in the end he merely said under his breath:

'Go and get dressed.'

They were disconcerted by that, Jenny even more than Gisèle. She opened her mouth to speak, said nothing and then decided, after giving her sister a harsh and hateful look, to go up the stairs first; as she climbed, Maigret could see her naked, white thighs.

'You too . . .'

In a slightly husky voice, Gisèle said:

'I know.'

She seemed to be waiting for her sister to close the door of her room before going upstairs.

Maigret stayed on his own with Marton's corpse for only a few moments and barely had time to look around and take stock of the room. Nevertheless, it was photographed in his mind, down to the slightest details, and he knew he would find them in his memory when he needed them.

He heard a car pull up, a squeak of brakes, the slamming of a door. Then there were footsteps in the courtyard, and, as Lapointe had done for him, he opened the door.

He knew Boisset, the inspector of the fourteenth arrondissement, who was accompanied by a uniformed officer and a chubby little man carrying a doctor's bag.

'Come in, all three of you . . . I think, doctor, that all you have to do is record the death . . . Doctor Paul will be here shortly . . .'

Boisset looked at him quizzically.

'A case I've been looking into for two days,' Maigret murmured. 'I'll explain later . . . For now, there's nothing to be done.'

They heard footsteps above their heads, a tap being turned on, a toilet being flushed.

As Boisset looked up at the ceiling in surprise, Maigret went on:

'The wife and the sister-in-law . . .'

He felt as weary as if it was he, and not Lapointe, who had spent the night outside, in the cold and rain. Lapointe would be back shortly. The doctor, after kneeling down for a moment, got back to his feet. He had pointed a torch at the dead man's staring eyes, then brought his face close to the man's lips and sniffed.

'At first sight, it looks like a poisoning.'

'It is.'

Lapointe gestured to Maigret to say that he had fulfilled his mission. Whispering was heard in the courtyard. Several people had approached the shutters, which were still closed.

Maigret said to the uniformed officer:

'You should go outside and disperse any people who have gathered.'

The doctor asked:

'Do you still need me?'

'No. Later we'll give you the information you need on the man's identity for the death certificate.'

'Goodbye, gentlemen! Boisset knows where to find me . . .'

Gisèle Marton came downstairs first, and Maigret noticed immediately that she was wearing her suit and had her fur coat over her arm. She was also holding a handbag, which suggested that she expected to be led away. She had taken the time to put on her make-up, and discreetly. The expression on her face was grave, thoughtful, still with a hint of surprise.

When Jenny appeared in turn, she was wearing a black dress. Noticing her sister's outfit, she asked, after moistening her lips:

'Will I need a coat?'

Maigret blinked. The one who was observing him most intensely was Lapointe, who had rarely been so impressed by his attitude. He felt that this was no ordinary investigation, and that the chief had no intention of proceeding in a normal fashion, but he hadn't the faintest idea what he planned to do.

His nerves were so tense that it was a relief to see Bois-set light a cigarette. He held out his pack to Lapointe, who declined, then, turning to Gisèle, who was waiting as if on a station platform, averting her eyes from the dead man, he said:

'Do you smoke?'

She took one. He brought the flame of his lighter closer, and she inhaled nervously.

'Do you have a police car by the door?' Maigret asked the local inspector.

'I kept it just in case.'

'Can I use it?'

He was still looking around him, as if to check that he hadn't forgotten a single detail. He was about to give the two women the sign that they were leaving when he changed his mind.

'Just a moment . . .'

And he in turn went upstairs, to the first floor, where the lights were still lit. There were only two bedrooms, a bathroom and a box room piled high with suitcases, old trunks, a tailor's mannequin and old paraffin lamps on the floor along with some dusty books.

He went into the first bedroom, the larger of the two. It contained a double bed, and the smell told him that he was in Madame Marton's room. The wardrobe confirmed as much, because he found in it clothes of the kind he had seen her wearing: simple, elegant, even luxurious. On a board just above the floor a dozen pairs of shoes were lined up.

The bed was unmade, like the one downstairs. The nightdress had been thrown carelessly on it, along with the salmon-pink dressing gown. On the dressing table there were pots of cream, some little bottles, a silver manicure set and pins in a Chinese bowl.

In another wardrobe there were men's clothes: only two suits, a sports jacket, two pairs of shoes and some espadrilles. There mustn't have been a wardrobe downstairs, and Marton still kept his belongings in the marital bedroom.

He looked in the chests of drawers, pushed open a door and found himself in the bathroom. On the glass tray he saw three tooth mugs, a brush in each, which indicated that each of them came to the room in turn. Some lipstick on crumpled napkins, one of which had been thrown on the floor. And on the porcelain toilet bowl and the tiles surrounding it, there were little dried stains, as if someone had been vomiting during the night.

The other room did not open on to the bathroom. It had to be reached via the corridor. It was smaller, papered with blue floral wallpaper, and the bed was a single one.

This room was untidier than the other. The wardrobe door hadn't been closed. A tweed coat bore the label of a New York fashion house. Not nearly as many shoes, only four pairs, two of them also from America. Last of all, on the table covered with an embroidered cloth which served as a dressing table, a collection of disparate objects: a pencil with a broken lead, a ballpoint pen, some change, some combs, some hairpins, a brush that had lost some of its bristles.

Maigret recorded it all. When he came back down he was just as torpid as before, and with staring eyes.

He discovered that the kitchen was on the ground floor, behind a partition that had been put up in a corner of what had been a carpenter's workshop. He pushed the door open, while Gisèle Marton kept her eyes on him. It had a gas hob, a white food cupboard, a sink and a table covered with a waxed tablecloth.

There was no washing-up lying around. The porcelain of the sink was dry.

He went back to the others, who still stood frozen as if in a wax museum.

'You will receive these gentlemen from the prosecutor's office,' he said to Lapointe. 'Apologize to Doctor Paul on my behalf for not waiting for him. Ask him to call me as soon as he has done what needs to be done. I'm going to send you someone, I don't yet know who . . .'

He turned towards the two women.

'If you would follow me . . .'

Of the two, the sister-in-law was the more frightened, and it seemed as if she was repelled by the idea of leaving the house. Gisèle, on the other hand, had opened the door, and was standing stiffly waiting in the rain.

The police officer had driven away the onlookers in the courtyard, but was unable to stop them forming a circle at the end of the alley, on the pavement. The old woman was still there, her purple shawl on her head as an umbrella. The Métro employee must have gone regretfully to work.

They were looking at them the way the public always

looks at comings and goings which look both mysterious and dramatic. The policeman parted the crowd to allow access to the car, and Maigret ushered the two women ahead of him.

A voice said:

'He's arresting them . . .'

He closed the door behind them and walked around the car to take his seat beside the uniformed driver.

'To the Police Judiciaire.'

The day was beginning to dawn, however vaguely. The rain was turning grey, the sky dirty. They overtook buses, and half-awake people were dashing down the stairs into the Métro.

By the time they reached the river the streetlamps barely gave off any light, and the towers of Notre Dame stood out against the sky.

The car drove into the courtyard. On the way, the two women hadn't said a word, but one of them, Jenny, had sniffed several times. Once she had spent a long time blowing her nose. When she got out of the car her nose was red, as Marton's had been on his first visit.

'This way, please.'

He walked ahead of them up the big staircase, which was just being swept, pushed open the glass-panelled door and looked around for Joseph but couldn't see him. At last he showed them into his office, where he turned on the lights, looking briefly in on the inspectors' office; there were only three of them in there, three who knew nothing about the case.

He chose Janin at random.

'Will you stay in my office with these ladies for a moment?'

And, turning towards them:

'Please, take a seat. I assume you haven't had any coffee?'

Jenny didn't reply. Madame Marton shook her head.

Maigret walked ostentatiously to the door, locked it from inside and put the key in his pocket.

'It would be a good idea to take a seat,' he said again, 'because you'll be here for a while.'

He went into the other office.

'Baron! Phone the Brasserie Dauphine. Tell them to bring a big pot of coffee . . . Black coffee . . . Three cups and some croissants . . .'

After which he slumped on a chair, near the window, picked up another receiver and asked for the private number of the public prosecutor. He would just have got up and right now he would probably be getting dressed and having his breakfast. And yet it wasn't a servant who answered, but the prosecutor himself.

'Maigret here, sir . . . Marton is dead . . . The man I told you about yesterday morning. No, I'm at Quai des Orfèvres . . . I left an inspector at Avenue de Châtillon, Lapointe . . . Doctor Paul has been alerted . . . So has Criminal Records, yes . . . I don't know . . . The two women are in my office . . .'

He spoke in a low voice, even though the connecting door between the two rooms was closed.

'I don't think I can go there this morning . . . I'll send another inspector to take over from Lapointe . . .'

He almost looked guilty. Once the call was over he looked at his watch and chose to wait for Janvier, who would be there soon, and who knew about the case.

After running his hands over his cheeks, he asked the third inspector, Bonfils, who was busy writing his report on the events of the evening:

'Would you go to my cupboard and find my razor, my shaving soap and my towel?'

He preferred not to do that in front of the two women. Holding his washing implements, he walked to the corridor and went into the toilets, where he took off his jacket and shaved. He took his time, as if to put off the moment when he would have to do what he still had to do. Having splashed cold water on his face, he returned to his colleagues and the waiter from the Brasserie Dauphine, who didn't know where to set down his tray.

'In my office . . . Over here . . .'

He picked up the phone again, and this time he spoke to his wife.

'I'm going to have a busy morning. I don't yet know if I'll be home for lunch.'

His tired voice worried her:

'Has something bad happened?'

What could he say?

'Don't worry. I'm about to have my breakfast.'

Finally, he said to Bonfils:

'When Janvier comes, tell him to come and see me.'

He went into his office, which the coffee-waiter was just leaving, and let Janin go. Then, as if in slow motion or in a dream, he poured coffee into the three cups.

'Sugar?' he asked Gisèle first of all.

'Two, please.'

He held out the cup and the plate of croissants, but she gestured that she didn't want to eat.

'Sugar?'

The sister-in-law shook her head. She didn't eat either, and he was the only one who nibbled on a warm croissant without much of an appetite.

The day had broken, but it was still too dim to turn out the lights. Twice more, Jenny had opened her mouth to ask a question, but had given up both times at the sight of Maigret's expression.

The time had come. Maigret, who had poured himself a second cup of coffee, was slowly filling a pipe that he had chosen from among the pipes scattered on his desk.

Then, still standing, he looked at the women in turn.

'I think I'll start with you,' he murmured, stopping at Madame Marton.

Jenny gave a start and, once again, wanted to say something.

'As for you, I would like you to wait in another room with one of my inspectors.'

He called Janin back.

'Please take this lady to the green office and stay with her until I call you.'

It wasn't the first time this had happened. They were used to it.

'Certainly, chief.'

'Isn't Janvier here yet?'

'I think I heard his voice in the corridor.'

'Tell him to come straight away.'

Janin left with the sister-in-law. Janvier came in a moment later and stopped with surprise as he recognized Madame Marton sitting on a chair, holding a cup of coffee.

'Marton is dead,' Maigret announced. 'Lapointe is at the scene. He spent the night there and it would be a good idea to go and relieve him.'

'No orders, chief?'

'Lapointe will give you your instructions. If you take a car, you'll get there before the prosecutors do.'

'You're not coming?'

'I don't think so.'

At last the two doors were closed, and Maigret and Madame Marton were left alone in the office. It seemed as if she too had been waiting for that moment, and while he remained silent in front of her, puffing on his pipe, she grew slowly animated and began to shed some of her torpor, or rather her tension.

It was curious to see her face turning human again, her skin colouring slightly, her eyes expressing something other than waiting.

'You think I poisoned him, don't you?'

He took his time. It wasn't the first time he had avoided, as he had just done, asking questions at the moment a crime had been revealed. It is often preferable to avoid making people talk too quickly, whether suspects or witnesses, because once they have spoken they feel they have to stick to what they said for fear that they will be accused of lying.

He had deliberately given them both time to think, to decide on their attitudes and the statements they would make.

'I don't think anything,' he murmured at last. 'You'll notice that I didn't bring in the officer who takes shorthand. I won't record what you say to me. Just tell me simply what happened.'

He knew she was disconcerted by his calm demeanour and his simple way of speaking.

'Let's start with yesterday evening, for example.'

'What do you want to know?'

'Everything.'

It was awkward. She was wondering where to start her story, and he helped her along a little.

'You went home . . .'

'As I do every evening, obviously.'

'At what time?'

'Eight o'clock. After the shop shut, I went for a drink in a bar on Rue Castiglione.'

'With Monsieur Harris?'

'Yes.'

'And then?'

'My husband came home before I did. My sister was home as well. We sat down to eat.'

'Was it your sister who made dinner?'

'As always.'

'You eat downstairs, in the living room, which is both your husband's workshop and bedroom?'

'He decided to sleep there some months ago.'

'How many months?'

She counted mentally. Her lips moved.

'Eight months,' she said at last.

'What did you have?'

'Soup first of all . . . The same as the previous day . . . Jenny always makes soup for two days . . . Then some ham and salad, cheese and pears . . .'

'Coffee?'

'We never have coffee in the evening.'

'You didn't notice anything unusual?'

She hesitated, looking him straight in the eyes.

'That depends what you call unusual. I don't know exactly what to say to you, because I suspect there are some things that you know better than me. The proof is that there was an inspector at the door. Before going to sit at the table I got up to take off my coat and put on my slippers. That's how I knew that my sister had gone out, and that she had only just come back.'

'How did you know?'

'Because I opened the door of her room and saw a pair of shoes that were still wet. Her coat was damp, too.'

'What were you going to do in her room?'

'Just check that she had gone out.'

'Why?'

Still without looking away, she replied:

'To know.'

'Jenny cleared the table?'

'Yes.'

'Does she always clear it?'

'She likes to pay her share by looking after the housework.'

'And did she do the washing-up as well?'

'Sometimes my husband helps her.'

'Not you?'

'No.'

'Go on.'

'She made the herbal tea, as she did on the other evenings. She was the one who got us used to drinking herbal tea in the evening.'

'Lime-flower? Camomile?'

'No. Star anise. My sister has a weak liver. Since living in the United States, she has a cup of star anise every evening, and my husband wanted to try it, I didn't. You know how it is . . .'

'She brought in the cups on a tray?'

'Yes.'

'With the teapot?'

'No. She filled the cups in the kitchen and then came and set the tray down on the table.'

'What was your husband doing at that moment?'

'He was looking for a radio station.'

'So if I remember the room correctly, he had his back towards you?'

'Yes.'

'What were you doing?'

'I had just started reading a magazine.'

'Near the table?'

'Yes.'

'And your sister?'

'She went back into the kitchen to start doing the washing-up. I know what you're getting at, but I'll tell you the truth anyway. I didn't pour any substance into the cups, either into my husband's or into the others. All I did was take a precaution that I've been taking for some time whenever possible.'

'What was that?'

'To turn the tray discreetly in such a way that the cup meant for me becomes my husband's or my sister's.'

'And last night, your cup became . . .'

'My husband's.'

'And he took it?'

'Yes. He took it with him and then set it down on the radio . . .'

'You never left the room at any time? There couldn't have been any other substitution?'

'I've been thinking about that for almost two hours.'

'What conclusion did you reach?'

'Before my sister brought the tray, my husband went into the kitchen. Jenny will probably deny it, but it's the truth.'

'What did he go there to do?'

'By his account, to see if his glasses were there. He wears glasses to read. He also needs them to see the screen of the radio. From the studio you can hear everything that's going on in the kitchen. He didn't talk to my sister, he came back almost immediately and found his glasses near the train set.'

'And it was because of this visit to the kitchen that you swapped the cups around?'

'Perhaps. Not necessarily. I told you, I do it often.'

'Because you're afraid he's going to poison you?'

She looked at him without replying.

'Then what happened?'

'Nothing different from the other evenings. My sister came back to drink her herbal tea and went back into the kitchen. Xavier listened to a radio programme while repairing a little electric motor intended for God knows what.'

'And you read?'

'For an hour or two. It was about ten o'clock when I went upstairs.'

'You went first?'

'Yes.'

'What was your sister doing at that point?'

'She was making my husband's bed.'

'You usually left them alone?'

'Why not? What difference would it have made?'

'Do you think they took advantage of the fact to kiss?'

'I don't care.'

'Do you have reason to believe that your husband was your sister's lover?'

'I don't know if they were lovers. I doubt it. He behaved with her like a smitten seventeen-year-old.'

'Why did you just say: "I doubt it"?'

She didn't reply immediately. At last, in response to Maigret's insistent gaze, she answered his question with another question.

'Why do you think we don't have children?'

'Because you didn't want to.'

'That's what he told you, isn't it? And it's probably what he told his colleagues. A man doesn't like to admit that he's practically impotent.'

'Is that the case?'

She nodded wearily.

'You see, inspector, there are lots of things you don't know. Xavier gave you his version of our lives. When I came to see you, I didn't take the trouble to go into details. Things happened last night that I don't understand, and I know that when I tell you, you won't believe me.'

He didn't push her. On the contrary, he gave her all the time in the world to speak and even to weigh her phrases.

'I heard the doctor just now saying that Xavier had been poisoned. Perhaps it's true. But I have been too.'

He couldn't help giving a start and looking at her more keenly.

'You've been poisoned?'

A memory came back to him, one which inclined him to believe her: the stains that had already dried on the porcelain of the basin and the tiles.

'I woke up in the middle of the night with horrible burning in my stomach. When I got up I was surprised to feel my legs were weak, my head empty. I hurried to the bathroom and stuck two fingers into my mouth to vomit. I'm sorry if that puts you off your food. It was like fire, with an aftertaste that I would recognize anywhere.'

'Did you alert your sister or your husband?'

'No. Perhaps they heard me, because I flushed the toilet twice. I made myself sick twice too, each time spitting out a liquid that had the same aftertaste.'

'It didn't occur to you to call a doctor?'

'What would be the point? Since I had caught it in time . . .'

'You went back to bed?'

'Yes.'

'You weren't tempted to go back downstairs?'

'I just listened. I heard Xavier tossing and turning in his bed as if he was sleeping badly.'

'Do you think it was his cup that you drank from?'

'I assume so.'

'You still insist that you swapped the cups around on the tray?'

'Yes.'

'And then you didn't take your eyes off the tray? Your husband, or your sister, couldn't have made another substitution?'

'My sister was in the kitchen.'

'So your husband took the cup that was meant for you?'

'I would have to believe that.'

'Which is to say that it was your sister who tried to poison your husband?'

'I don't know.'

'Or since your husband was poisoned as well, she wanted to poison both of you?'

She repeated:

'I don't know.'

They looked at each other in silence for a long time. In the end it was Maigret who broke eye contact and went and stood by the window, where, watching the Seine flow beneath the rain, he filled a fresh pipe.

8. A Mark on the Tray

Pressing his forehead against the cold glass, as he had done when he was a child, keeping it there until his skin turned white and he felt pins and needles in his head, Maigret was unwittingly following the movements of two men working on scaffolding on the other side of the Seine.

When he turned around, his face bore a resigned expression and, as he made for his desk to sit back down in his chair, he said, deliberately avoiding Gisèle Marton's eyes:

'Is there something else you want to tell me?'

She didn't hesitate for very long, and, when she spoke, he couldn't help raising his head, because she did so in a calm and measured voice free of either defiance or despondency:

'I saw Xavier dying.'

Did she know the impression she was making on the inspector? Did she realize that she was inspiring in him an involuntary, so to speak technical admiration? He couldn't remember seeing, in this office through which so many people had passed, a creature with such clarity and level-headedness. Neither could he remember anyone so *detached*.

There was no sense in her of human feeling. There was no flaw.

With his elbows on his desk-blotter, he sighed:

'Tell me.'

'I had gone to bed and was having trouble getting back to sleep. I was struggling to understand what had happened. I had no real notion of passing time. You know how that happens sometimes. You have a sense of following a continuous train of thought, but in fact there are gaps. I must have gone back to sleep several times. Once or twice I thought there was a noise downstairs, the noise my husband made when he turned over abruptly in bed. At least that was what I thought.

'Once, I'm sure, I heard a groan and thought he must be having nightmares. It wasn't the first time he had spoken and thrashed about in his sleep. He told me that as a boy he had sleepwalked, and that happened to him several times with me.'

She went on choosing her words, without any more emotion than if she was telling a story.

'At one point I heard a louder noise, as if something heavy was falling on the floor. I was too frightened to get up at first. Pricking up my ears, I thought I heard a death rattle. Then I got up, put on my dressing gown and walked silently towards the stairs.'

'Did you see your sister?'

'No.'

'Or hear a sound in her room? There was no light under her door?'

'No. To look into the room downstairs I had to go down a few steps, and I hesitated, alert to potential danger. I still did it, reluctantly. I leaned down.'

'How many steps did you go down?'

'Six or seven. I didn't count them. There was a light on in the workshop, only the bedside lamp. Xavier was lying on the floor, about halfway between his bed and the spiral staircase. It looked as if he had been crawling, as if he was trying to crawl some more. He had raised himself up on one elbow, his left elbow, and his right arm was stretched out to pick up the revolver that was about thirty centimetres away from his hand.'

'Did he see you?'

'Yes. With his head raised, he stared at me with hatred, his face contorted, with foam or drool on his lips. I realized that, while he was walking towards the stairs, already weakened, with his gun in his hand, to come up to kill me, his strength had failed him, he had fallen, and the revolver had rolled out of reach.'

With his eyes half closed, Maigret saw the workshop again, the staircase that rose towards the ceiling, Marton's body as they had found it.

'Did you continue down the stairs?'

'No. I stayed where I was, unable to take my eyes off him. I couldn't know exactly how much energy he still had. I was fascinated.'

'How long did it take him to die?'

'I don't know. He was trying to grab the gun and talk to me at the same time, to shout out his hatred or his threats. At the same time he was scared that I would come down, that I would pick up the gun before he did and fire. That's probably partly the reason why I didn't go down. I don't really know. I wasn't thinking. He was panting. He was shaken by spasms. I thought he was going to vomit as I had done. Then he uttered a loud cry, his body was shaken several times, he clenched his hands and at last, all of a sudden, he was still.'

Without looking away, she said:

'I knew it was over.'

'And it was then that you went downstairs to check that he was dead?'

'No. I knew he was. I don't know why I was so sure of it. I went back up to my room and sat down on the edge of my bed. I was cold. I wrapped the blanket around my shoulders.'

'Your sister still hadn't left her room?'

'No.'

'And yet you just said he had uttered a loud cry.'

'That's right. She must have heard it. She couldn't have helped hearing it, but she stayed in her bed.'

'You didn't think of calling a doctor? Or phoning the police?'

'Had there been a telephone in the house, I might have done. I'm not sure.'

'What time was it?'

'I don't know. It didn't occur to me to check my alarm-clock. I was still trying to understand.'

'If you had had a telephone, wouldn't you have called your friend Harris?'

'Certainly not. He's married.'

'So you don't know, even approximately, how much time passed between the moment you saw your husband die and the one when, at about six o'clock in the morning, you went and called from the concierge's lodge? Was it one hour? Two hours? Three?'

'More than an hour, I would swear. Less than three.'

'Did you expect to be accused?'

'I was under no illusions.'

'And you were wondering how you would answer the questions you would be asked?'

'It's possible. Without realizing, I thought a lot. Then I heard the familiar sound of the bins being dragged into a nearby courtyard and I went downstairs.'

'Still without meeting your sister?'

'Yes. In passing, I touched my husband's hand. It was already cold. I looked up your phone number in the directory, and when I didn't find it I called the Police Emergency Service to ask them to inform you.'

'After which you went back home?'

'I saw the light in my sister's room from the courtyard. When I pushed the door open, Jenny was coming down the stairs.'

'Had she already seen the body?'

'Yes.'

'And she didn't say anything?'

'She might have spoken if there hadn't been a sudden knock at the door. It was your inspector.'

She added after a pause:

'If there's any coffee left . . .'

'It's cold.'

'That doesn't matter.'

He poured her a cup, and also poured one for himself.

Beyond the door, beyond the window, life went on, everyday life, the way people have organized it as a source of reassurance.

Here, in these four walls, it was a different world that you could sense throbbing behind sentences, behind words, a dark and unsettling world, but one in which this young woman seemed to move easily.

'Did you love Marton?' Maigret asked under his breath, almost in spite of himself.

'No. I don't think so.'

'And yet you married him.'

'I was twenty-eight. I was fed up with all my failed attempts.'

'You wanted respectability?'

She didn't seem offended.

'Calm, at any rate.'

'Did you choose Marton in preference over others because he was more malleable?'

'Perhaps unconsciously.'

'Did you already know that he was more or less impotent?'

'Yes. That wasn't what I was looking for.'

'At first you were happy with him?'

'That's a big word. We got on quite well.'

'Because he did what you wanted?'

She pretended not to notice the hint of aggression in his voice, or the way he looked at her.

'I never asked myself that question.'

Nothing threw her, and yet she was beginning to show a little weariness.

'When you met Harris or, if you prefer, Maurice Schwob, did you love him?'

She thought for a moment, with a kind of honesty, as if she was keen to be precise.

'You're still using that word. First of all, Maurice was able to change my situation, and I never thought my place was behind the counter of a large department store.'

'Did he become your lover straight away?'

'That depends on what you mean by straight away. A few days, if I remember correctly. Neither of us placed much importance on it.'

'So your relationship was built on business more than anything else?'

'If you like. I know that between two hypotheses you're going to choose the more sordid one. I'll say instead that Maurice and I felt we were two of a kind . . .'

'Because you had the same ambitions. It never occurred to you to get a divorce in order to marry him?'

'What would have been the point? He is married, to an older woman, who has money, and who enabled him to set up the shop on Rue Saint-Honoré. And as to the rest . . .'

The rest, she implied, was of no importance.

'When did you begin to suspect that your husband was losing his mind? Because you did have that impression, didn't you?'

'It wasn't an impression, it was a certainty. From the beginning, I knew he wasn't exactly like anyone else. He had periods of exaltation, in which he talked about his work as a genius might have done, and others when he complained of being a failure that everyone laughed at.'

'Including you.'

'Of course. I think I know that it was always like that. During that last period he was gloomy and anxious, he observed me with suspicion, before exploding into rebukes when I least expected it. Other times, on the contrary, he operated by insinuation.'

'Didn't that make you want to leave him?'

'I think I was sorry for him. He was unhappy. When my sister arrived from the United States, in full mourning, playing the part of the inconsolable widow, he avoided her at first. She disturbed his habits, and he couldn't forgive her; he spent whole days not addressing a word to her.

'I still wonder how she managed to win him over. What did seem to work was making herself look forlorn.

'So, he suddenly had someone weaker than him in his power. At least that was what he thought. Do you understand? With my sister, he had a sense of being a man, a solid and superior being . . .'

'You still didn't think of divorcing him to give them a free hand?'

'They would have been miserable together in any case, because my sister isn't really so weak – quite the contrary.'

'Do you hate her?'

'We've never liked each other.'

'In that case, why did you take her in?'

'Because she imposed herself.'

If Maigret felt a weight on his shoulders, and had a bad taste in his mouth, it was because he sensed it was all true.

The atmosphere in the house on Avenue de Châtillon would indeed have been as described so succinctly by Madame Marton, and he could imagine the almost silent evenings during which each of them remained wrapped up in their hatred.

'What were you hoping? That it wouldn't last for long?'

'I went to see a doctor.'

'Steiner?'

'No. Another one. I told him everything.'

'And he didn't advise you to have your husband committed?'

'He advised me to wait, telling me that the symptoms weren't yet well enough defined, that a more violent crisis would occur in due course . . .'

'So you predicted that crisis and stayed on the alert?'

She shrugged very slightly.

'Have I answered all your questions?' she asked after a short silence.

Maigret tried to think and couldn't come up with anything else to ask, because almost everything had been cleared up.

'When you stopped on the stairs and saw your husband on the floor, you didn't try to help him?'

'I didn't know if he had the strength to pick up the revolver . . .'

'You're sure that your sister was aware of everything you've just told me?'

She looked at him without replying.

What was the point of going on? He would have liked to make her contradict herself. He would have liked to accuse her. She didn't lay herself open. But neither did she hide herself away.

'I assume,' he murmured, shooting one last arrow, 'that you have never had any intention of getting rid of your husband?'

'By killing him?'

She was marking the distinction between killing him and having him committed. Since he said yes, she announced simply:

'If I had had to kill him, I would have left nothing to chance and I wouldn't be here now.'

That was true. If anyone was capable of committing a perfect crime, it was this woman.

Unfortunately she hadn't killed Marton, and after relighting his pipe and looking at her grudgingly, Maigret rose heavily to his feet, his body and mind numb, and headed towards the door of the inspectors' office.

'Have somebody call 17, Avenue de Châtillon . . . The concierge's lodge . . . Janvier is in the house at the end of the courtyard . . . I'd like to have a word with him . . .'

He came back to his chair, and while he waited she put a little powder on her face, as she might have done at the theatre during the interval. The telephone had rung at last.

'Janvier . . . ? I'd like you to go into the house, without hanging up, and carefully examine a tray that must be in the kitchen . . .'

He turned towards Gisèle Marton.

'A round or a square tray?'

'A rectangular tray, made of wood.'

'A wooden tray, rectangular, big enough to carry three cups and three saucers . . . What I want to know is whether there's any kind of mark, a scratch, any sign that would tell us if the tray is set down in one direction or another . . . You see what I mean . . . ? Just a moment . . . The experts are still there? . . . Good! . . . Ask them to look for a little bottle in the broom cupboard, containing a whitish powder . . . and take fingerprints . . .'

Janvier was able to answer the second question straight away.

'There are no prints. They've already checked. The bottle was wiped with a damp and slightly greasy cloth, probably a dishcloth.'

'Did people from the prosecutor's office arrive?'

'Yes. The examining magistrate isn't happy.'

'Because I didn't wait for him?'

'Mostly because you took away the two women.'

'Tell him that by the time he gets to his office it will probably be over. Which judge is it?'

'Coméliau.'

The two men couldn't stand each other.

'Go and take a quick look at the tray. I'll stay on the line.'

He heard the voice of Gisèle Marton, to whom he hadn't been paying attention.

'If you'd asked me, I could have told you. There's a mark. It wasn't made on purpose. The varnish has formed a blister on one of the short sides of the rectangle.'

A few moments later, Janvier, slightly out of breath, said to him:

'There's a swelling in the varnish.'

'Thank you. Nothing else?'

'In Marton's pocket they found a bit of crumpled paper that had contained zinc phosphide.'

'I know.'

Not that the paper would be in the dead man's pocket, but that they would find it somewhere in the room.

He hung up.

'When you saw your husband going into the kitchen, you suspected what he was going to do, didn't you? That's why you swapped the cups around?'

'I swapped them around whenever I could.'

'Did he sometimes swap them as well?'

'He certainly did. Except yesterday evening he couldn't, because I didn't take my eyes off the tray.'

At Boulevard Richard-Lenoir as well there was a tray, not made of wood, but of silver plate, a wedding present. Maigret's cup and his wife's were the same, except that his had a barely visible crack.

And yet they never got them muddled. When Madame Maigret put the tray down on the table, near her husband's armchair, he would know that his own cup was on his side, within hand's reach.

He had got up once more. Madame Marton watched him, curious but not anxious.

'Will you come here for a moment, Lucas? Find an empty office, any one will do, and go there with her. Stay there until I call you. On the way, tell them to bring in the sister-in-law.'

Madame Marton followed Lucas without asking

Maigret a single question. Once he was on his own, he opened his cupboard, took out the bottle of cognac that he kept there, less for himself than for some of his clients who sometimes needed it, and poured some into the water glass.

When there was a knock at the door, he closed the cupboard door and only just had time to wipe his lips.

'Come in!'

Jenny was brought in, her face pale and swollen, with the red marks of someone who has been crying.

'Take a seat.'

The chair where her sister had been sitting was still warm. Jenny looked around, disconcerted to find herself on her own with the inspector.

He remained standing, pacing back and forth, uncertain how to attack, and at last, standing in front of her, he said:

'Which lawyer are you going to choose?'

She lifted her head abruptly, her eyes wide and moist. Her lips were moving, but she couldn't speak.

'I would rather question you in the presence of your lawyer, so that you don't feel that I'm setting traps for you.'

'I don't know any lawyers.'

He took down a directory from the bookshelf and held it out to her.

'Choose from this list.'

She shook her head.

'What's the point?'

How he wished it had been the other one!

'You confess?'

She nodded, rummaged in her handbag for her handkerchief and blew her nose inelegantly, making it even redder.

'You admit that you planned to poison your sister?'

Then she burst into a fit of sobs.

'I don't know any more . . . Don't torture me . . . I just want it all to be over . . .'

She was shaken by hiccups. It didn't occur to her to hide her wet face.

'Did you love your brother-in-law?'

'I don't know. I don't know any more. I suppose so . . .'

Her eyes were pleading.

'Please get it over with, inspector! I can't bear it any more . . .'

And now that he knew, he made it as quick as possible. He even, in passing, touched the young woman's shoulder, as if he knew that she needed human contact.

'You realized that Xavier wasn't like other people?'

She nodded. She shook her head. She was battling with problems that were too complicated for her, and at last she exclaimed:

'She was the one who didn't understand him, and who was driving him mad . . .'

'On purpose?'

'I don't know. He needed . . .'

The words struggled to come.

'I tried . . .'

'To reassure him?'

'You can't know what an atmosphere we were living

in . . . It was only when we were alone, he and I . . . Because with me he felt at ease, confident . . .'

'When he joined you by the river, yesterday evening, did he tell you that he was to come and take a test this morning?'

Surprised that Maigret knew about it, she sat there for a moment, looking at him open-mouthed.

'Give me an answer . . . I'm trying to deliver you as quickly as possible as well . . .'

She understood the word. She didn't imagine that he was talking about giving her back her freedom, but rather that he was talking about delivering her from herself in some sense.

'He told me,' she admitted reluctantly.

'He was frightened about it?'

She said yes, sniffing, and added, again on the point of tears:

'He imagined that she had won . . .'

The choice of words betrayed the chaos in her thoughts.

'Because she was the one who drove him to all that. She had made sure that he would find the poison, that he would get ideas . . .'

'Did he hate her?'

She stared at him fearfully, without daring to reply.

'And so did you, isn't that right? You began to hate your sister?'

She shook her head. It didn't mean either yes or no. She was in fact trying to dispel the nightmare.

'Last night, when you left here,' Maigret went on, 'Marton imagined that after his medical examination he wouldn't be freed . . . So he only had one evening . . . That was his last chance . . .'

The behaviour of the toy salesman might have appeared incoherent, but it did contain a certain logic, and Maigret was beginning to understand certain passages in the psychiatric textbook. Except that what the author of the book expressed in difficult language and complicated phrases was in the end merely human.

'When he went to the kitchen while you were there . . .'

She shivered, wanting him to be quiet.

'The herbal tea was already in the cups?'

He was sure of it and didn't need an answer.

'Did you see him pouring in the powder?'

'I had my back to him. He opened the cutlery drawer and took out a knife. I heard him rummaging among the knives . . .'

'And you thought he didn't have the courage to pour in the poison?'

Maigret saw the knife again, with its dark wood handle, beside the radio, which had a catalogue lying on top of it.

Beneath Maigret's serious gaze, Jenny wrestled with herself a little before groaning:

'I felt sorry . . .'

He could have replied:

'Not for your sister, at any rate?'

And she went on:

'I was sure he was going to be committed, that Gisèle had won the game . . . So . . .'

'So you picked up the bottle of phosphide and poured

a good dose into your sister's cup. You had the presence of mind to wipe the bottle.'

'I was holding a wet towel.'

'You checked that the cup meant for your sister was on the right side of the tray.'

'Please, inspector . . . ! If you knew the night I've had . . .'

'You heard everything?'

'How could I not have done?'

'And you didn't come downstairs?'

'I was too frightened.'

She was shivering in retrospect, and it was for her that he opened the cupboard again.

'Drink this.'

She obeyed, choked and almost spat out the cognac, which stung her throat.

It seemed that she had reached the point where she wanted to get down on the floor and lie there motionless without hearing another word.

'If only your brother-in-law had told you everything . . .'

Having collected herself, she wondered what she was going to hear now.

And Maigret, who remembered the words that Xavier Marton had uttered in this very office, explained:

'He didn't plan to get rid of his wife or take his revenge on her with poison, but with his revolver.'

Hadn't he almost succeeded? Don't psychiatrists talk about the rigorous logic of certain lunatics?

It was into his cup, *his own* cup, that he had poured the phosphide while moving the knives about, so quickly that his sister-in-law, who had her back to him, had thought that he had given up at the last moment.

He had measured the dose so as to be ill enough to explain what he was going to do next, but not enough to die of it. Not for no reason he had been haunting public libraries for months, immersing himself in medical and chemical textbooks.

That was the dose that Gisèle Marton had had when she swapped the cups around on the tray, and she had only been slightly indisposed.

And had Jenny worked all of that out during the endless night that she had spent in her room, listening to the noises of the house?

The proof that she knew was that she hunched herself more and more on her chair, head lowered, and stammered as if she no longer had the strength to articulate:

'I was the one who killed him . . .'

He left her to her discomfort, avoiding making a noise, for fear of seeing her rolling on the floor, and then, on tiptoes, he went into the inspectors' office.

'Have her taken down . . . Be gentle . . . First to the infirmary . . .' he said.

He preferred not to do it himself. Standing in front of the window, he wasn't even concerned about which inspectors were heading towards his office.

It wasn't his fault. He couldn't have taken Marton to the psychiatrist the first time he came to see him. And the psychiatrist probably wouldn't have assumed responsibility for a committal.

There is a vague zone between responsibility and

irresponsibility, a domain of shadows into which it is dangerous to venture.

Two people at least had struggled there, while a third . . .

'What will we do with the other one, chief?'

He gave a start, turned around, looking at the vast inspectors' office like a man who has just returned from a long journey.

'Let her go.'

He had nearly said:

'Throw her the hell outside.'

He waited for his own office to be free. Then he went back into it, and finding a residue of strange smells, opened the window.

He was deeply inhaling the damp air when Lucas said behind him:

'I don't know if I did the right thing. Before she left, Madame Marton asked permission to make a phone call. I said yes, thinking that it might tell us something.'

'What did she say to him?'

'You know who she talked to?'

'Harris.'

'She calls him Maurice. She apologized for not having been there for the opening of the shop. She didn't give any details. She just said: "I'll tell you shortly . . ."'

Maigret closed the window and turned his back to it, and Lucas, after observing him for a moment, said anxiously:

'What is it, chief?'

'Nothing. What could there be? That's what she said, and she isn't a woman who makes mistakes. Right now, she's in a taxi, holding a little mirror in front of her nose and adjusting her make-up . . .'

He emptied his pipe into the ashtray.

'Call the prosecutor's office and, if Coméliau is back, tell him I'm coming to see him straight away.'

It was over for him. The rest was a matter for the judges, and he had no wish to be in their place.

INSPECTOR MAIGRET

OTHER TITLES IN THE SERIES

www.penguin.com